DARK JOURNEY

Midwife Maudie Bryant is used to stumbling across murder — but now that she is the mother of a little boy, she has vowed to leave any future crime-solving to her husband Dick, a policeman. However, death strikes too close to home when a wealthy local woman, Cora Beasley, is found strangled with a belt from Maudie's dress. To make matters worse, it is well known that Maudie believed 'the beastly woman was out to snare Dick'. Can Detective Sergeant Bryant help to solve the crime before Maudie is charged as a suspect?

Books by Catriona McCuaig
in the Linford Mystery Library:

THE MIDWIFE AND THE MURDER
BLOOD LINES
BLOOD MONEY
FACE FROM THE PAST
UNHOLY GROUND
FIRE IN THE VALLEY
A MIDWIFE'S CHRISTMAS

CATRIONA McCUAIG

DARK
JOURNEY

Complete and Unabridged

LINFORD
Leicester

First published in Great Britain

First Linford Edition
published 2016

A catalogue record for this book is available
from the British Library.

ISBN 978–1–4448–3060–6

Published by
F. A. Thorpe (Publishing)
Anstey, Leicestershire

Set by Words & Graphics Ltd.
Anstey, Leicestershire
Printed and bound in Great Britain by
T. J. International Ltd., Padstow, Cornwall

This book is printed on acid-free paper

1

The distressing little scene being played out in the Bryants' cottage on that fine June morning was very possibly being duplicated in a thousand other homes across the country. *What a performance*, Maudie Bryant thought, watching her son in the midst of a full-scale tantrum. Having just been released from his highchair, he had toddled towards the sideboard, reaching out his chubby little hands towards the biscuit tin, knowing full well what was inside. 'Chocky bick?' he asked, flashing a winning smile at his mother.

'No biscuits for you, my lad! You didn't finish your egg and soldiers. Naughty little boys who don't eat up their breakfast don't deserve treats.'

His face reddened, his mouth turned down, and he began to dance up and down in rage. *Patience, Maudie! Every mother of an almost-two-year-old goes through this, and most of them manage to survive.*

Their poor dog retreated behind the sofa and began emitting small woofs of dismay.

'What's all this?' Dick Bryant, who had been dressing for work, came into the room, frowning. 'What's the matter with him, Maudie?'

'He wants a biscuit,' she mouthed, 'and I won't let him have one. That's all.'

'Stop that at once, Charlie Bryant!'

Charlie's voice rose to a shriek. Dick reached down and smacked his son on his well-padded bottom. The noise level subsided, and two fat tears rolled down the baby's chubby little cheeks.

'Dick Bryant! I can't believe you smacked Charlie!' Maudie glared at her husband, her eyes flashing.

'I should jolly well think I did! What a fuss about nothing!'

She wasn't sure if he meant Charlie's carrying-on or her own reaction, but she couldn't let this pass. 'He's only a baby, Dick. All children go through this sort of thing at this point in their development. That's why it's known as the Terrible Twos. We just have to put up with it. The child is only trying to assert his independence. We mustn't crush his spirit.'

'Balderdash! He has to learn that he can't always have his own way. Give in to him now, and what will he be like when he's ten years old? Fifteen? Twenty?'

'You only say that because you're a policeman. Charlie won't turn into a bank robber just because I've let him have the occasional chocolate biscuit.'

Charlie had been listening to their exchange with interest, looking from one parent to the other; but now, hearing the magic words, he once more burst into an ear-splitting roar.

'Poor little chap! Come to Mummy!' Maudie offered, holding out her arms to him.

'No! Don't want Mummy! Want Dada!' Charlie staggered over to Dick, burying his egg-stained little face in his father's good trousers.

Dick regarded her smugly. 'There, do you see? My little tap on the bottom has done him no harm at all. I haven't given him a complex. He hasn't been blighted for life.'

Rover came out from behind the sofa, pushing his wet nose into Maudie's hand. 'Poor old fellow,' she told him. 'Did the nasty people frighten him, then?'

'Arf!' said Rover.

'At least *somebody* loves me,' she told him, tickling him behind the ear, which he adored.

'Yes, well, this is all very interesting, but I have to get going,' Dick said, gently detaching his son's fingers from his trouser leg. 'See you later, old girl. Unless something interesting crops up, I shouldn't be late home.'

As she followed him to the door, with Charlie balanced on her hip, Dick reached over to kiss her on the cheek. Charlie grasped his hair and gave it a yank that made him gasp.

'Steady on, old chum! Don't deprive me of my few remaining hairs!' Dick was by no means bald, but there was no doubt that his hair was thinning. He tended to be sensitive about it, yet at the same time he had vowed to Maudie that he would never be one of those men who carefully arranged a few remaining strands of hair over an obviously balding dome. Making the best of what you had was one thing; vanity was quite another.

'*Interesting!*' Maudie muttered, when the sound of the car being driven off had faded away. All right for some! Her husband was going out into a world where, as a police detective, he would have *interesting* cases to work on and puzzles to solve. At the very least he would spend the day with other adults, where the level of conversation was, if not particularly intelligent, at least more challenging than interacting with a balky toddler.

She loved Dick and she adored this naughty baby, and she wouldn't be without either one of them for all the treasures of the Orient, but she couldn't deny that the pair of them tied her down. She had loved her work as a nurse and midwife, but all that had come to an end when she married. During her time spent serving the community, she had also become involved in solving a few murders and other crimes, and that had given her great satisfaction. That was all in the past now.

★ ★ ★

Despite its Welsh-sounding name, the village of Llandyfan was actually in England, close to the border. For centuries, it had been a straggling sort of place, with cottages strung out along the road leading to what was known locally as the Big House, where the Lords of the Manor had lived. Since the war, a small hamlet of prefabricated homes had been built a mile or so from the village proper, and this temporary housing was scheduled to be replaced in due course by permanent dwellings. Meanwhile, the occupants were regarded with suspicion by the villagers, despite the fact that their only crime was to have been bombed out of their city homes or otherwise displaced by the recent war.

There was not a great deal to do in Llandyfan. There was the church, with the various organizations associated with it; the village school, which was a Church of England institution; and the health clinic, situated in the former gatehouse of the manor. There was the village shop-cum-post-office; one pub, the Spread Eagle,

6

that also let out rooms; and the Copper Kettle, a tearoom much patronized by local ladies. If you craved anything more, you had to take the bus to Midvale, twelve miles away.

Despite the lack of amenities, people made their own fun — if you could call it that. There was the Mothers' Union, the Women's Institute, and the Scouts and Cubs, Brownies and Guides. The men had their darts and their bowls, and some enthusiasts played cricket in summer.

Somehow, none of that appealed to Maudie. She couldn't attend the women's meetings with a toddler clinging to her leg: lady speakers and committee chairpersons were apt to get annoyed if interrupted by screams of infant rage. Nor could she volunteer as a Sunday school teacher or Brown Owl, because she never knew when Dick would be called away on work-related matters, leaving her alone to cope with their son.

Yes, she loved their Charlie to bits, but she couldn't deny that his arrival had radically changed her life. No more romantic evenings out with Dick — not that he had ever been keen on dancing or partying. A birdwatching ramble was more his style. Still, a night out at the pictures, followed by a candlelit meal, would have been something — except, what could they do with Charlie? You couldn't park a baby in the cloakroom with your hat and coat!

She had known about all that during the course of her work as a midwife, when other women had complained about their lack of stimulation while being kept out of the mainstream by family duties. She had privately thought of some of them as a lot of moaning Minnies, but now she knew better!

Perhaps when Charlie was a little older she would take the lead and organize some sort of baby-sitting rota, where mothers in turn could entertain other women's children, along with their own, to give parents a break. Maudie was sure that such a scheme would benefit everyone and be greatly appreciated by all.

Meanwhile, she would have to get Dick to run her over to the Midvale library some evening, where she could stock up on books by her favourite authors. Agatha Christie, of course, and Dorothy L. Sayers, and Ngaio Marsh. In the absence of local crimes to solve, she could at least enjoy them second-hand. Although she did wish that something would happen closer to home! She didn't want anybody to die, of course, but would relish a good old-fashioned crime of some other sort. It was no good wishing, though; Dick would soon step in to prevent her taking an interest. But she could get round that little problem, couldn't she? She had managed it before!

Maudie smiled at the very notion. She had no idea how soon that thought would come back to haunt her.

'Come on, Charlie; let's get that egg washed off your face,' she told him, kissing the top of his head.

'No!'

'You're waiting for me to bribe you, aren't you?'

'No!'

His mother laughed.

2

Maudie had always felt she had a lot in common with Princess Elizabeth, despite the fact that the monarch's elder daughter had grown up in palaces and castles. Maudie's people had lived in a terraced house, and were respectable working-class people of the kind who toiled for long hours to keep their heads above water.

As a teenager, Maudie had saved her pocket money to buy a scrapbook in which she saved newspaper clippings about the royal family, using a paste made from flour and water. Later on, pictures of the Little Princesses, as they were known, were the ones she liked best, showing Elizabeth and her younger sister Margaret Rose. The public were charmed to learn that the elder girl referred to herself as Lilibet before she could get her tongue round her name; and that, as Maudie's grandmother told anyone who would listen, was a good thing too, because the child was named after her mother, the lovely young Duchess of York, and it would be difficult having two Elizabeths under one roof. How would they know how to reply when anyone shouted for them? Maudie very much doubted whether anyone would dare to shout at the Duchess, or it would be into the Tower and off with his head!

When Princess Elizabeth was nine years old, her grandfather died. He was her 'Grandpa England', but to all his subjects he was George V. The nation was plunged into mourning, but Maudie barely noticed because she was a nurse by then, working long hours at the hospital where she had trained. Too exhausted when she came off duty to do anything more than soak her feet in a basin of hot water laced with mustard, she had little time to decide what she made of the behaviour of the new king, who was to be known as Edward VIII.

'What do you think of him?' a patient asked her. 'They say he's had mistresses galore. Isn't that dreadful?' The woman's eyes shone as she thought of the delicious scandal.

'He's never been married, so I suppose

he can please himself,' Maudie said. 'Can you roll over, Mrs Brown? I want to wash your back.'

'He'll have to get married now, though, won't he? He has to provide England with heirs, so there will be someone to follow after him.'

Maudie, thinking of her beloved scrapbook, agreed that it would be lovely to have a royal wedding. Sadly, the country erupted in scandal before such a thing could happen. Edward VIII fell in love with an American woman called Mrs Simpson — who had already been divorced twice, if you please!

'Of course he can't marry her,' said the indefatigable Mrs Brown, who was still at the hospital after many bedridden weeks. 'Divorce is against the Church, and he's Defender of the Faith. He'll have a job getting wed now. Who would want to take him on, knowing he's got a mistress hidden away that he won't give up?'

'Plenty of women, I expect, if it meant they were going to be Queen,' Maudie replied, but Mrs Brown thought differently.

'There's going to be trouble in paradise,

Nurse, you mark my words. Once that woman has her claws in him, she won't let go.'

And trouble there was. When the king learned that his ministers, the majority of his subjects and the Archbishop of Canterbury were all against him, he abdicated, saying that he would never be able to rule the country, or, indeed, his Empire, without the support of the woman he loved. Some of Maudie's nursing friends thought this was 'so romantic', but she didn't agree. She didn't like the look of the American woman, although she had to admit that she was very chic.

Edward's place was taken by his younger brother, who was crowned in Westminster Abbey in May 1937, taking the title of George VI. Maudie was thrilled with the latest picture in her scrapbook, clipped from a magazine, which showed the little princesses, splendid in ermine-trimmed mantles, with coronets on their pretty heads. Little Margaret Rose was only six years old, so it seemed possible that their parents would have more children; but, if no son appeared to take his place as the next king in due course, then Princess Elizabeth would rule some day. Maudie was enchanted by the thought.

Life moved on, another war came, and Maudie lost interest in her royal hobby — or so she believed. But then Elizabeth grew up and married her handsome prince, and the whole world sat up and took an interest. First came the royal wedding, which burst upon the grey aftermath of a long and terrible war like the sun coming out after a violent thunderstorm. It seemed that the whole world wanted to share the princess's joy. At the time, Maudie bought a commemorative biscuit tin with pictures of the happy couple on it. In fact, it was that very same tin which now fascinated Charlie so much because of the chocolate biscuits it held!

And it was because of Charlie that Maudie felt close to the princess again. In 1948, little Prince Charles was born, followed by his sister Anne two years later. And in 1951, along came Charles Richard Bryant! Who could fail to feel a kinship there?

Mind you, however it might have seemed, Charlie wasn't named after the prince. Dick's father, Sapper Charles Bryant, had died in Flanders when his son had just started school. His widow had never remarried, but devoted herself to rearing their son to be as good a man as his father would have wanted him to be.

Sometimes, Dick wondered if any man could have been as saintly as she always made him out to be, and as the years passed his memories of his father grew fainter; but when his own son was born, he was glad to carry on the tradition. Charles Bryant, buried far away beneath a white wooden cross, was commemorated not only on a marble memorial, but also through the tiny grandson he would never see.

Dick vowed that he would bring up his son to be worthy of the honour; and if that meant giving him a tap on the sit-me-down when he was naughty, so be it!

Time had moved on, and George VI, the reluctant king, passed away after a long period of ill health. The shy man had been greatly respected for his courage at stepping into the breach after his brother's defection, as had also been his wife who, by her love and support, had enabled him to carry on.

'It must be very awkward for the poor woman,' Joan Blunt had said to Maudie on the morning after the king's death. Although older, the vicar's wife was a great friend of Maudie, and they always chatted together about the news of the day — local or otherwise.

'What do you mean, awkward?'

'Well, she's been Queen for years, hasn't she? Queen Consort, that is. Now her own daughter is Queen, and she'll have to curtsey to her and walk three paces behind when they attend events together. Surely it's bad enough being widowed without losing your place in the scheme of things! She'll have to watch her daughter being crowned next year, knowing that nothing will ever be the same again.'

Now, in the spring of 1953, England was gripped by coronation fever: planning street parties for the children, among other things. Maudie was excited because Cora Beasley, who was as close to being lady of the manor as anyone could be in this modern age, was staging a party of her own. She had hired a television set and issued invitations to a number of people to come for the day to watch the doings at the Abbey. The Bryants were to be included.

'And don't worry about the little boy,' Mrs Beasley said. 'If he gets restless we can put him down to sleep somewhere. And you must bring Rover, too. You won't want him left alone in the cottage all day.'

So Maudie had that to look forward to. Of course, the television would show everything in black and white, which was not the same as being there; but it was something not to be missed, and far less trouble than going to London and camping out overnight in an effort to be part of it all. Two nurses from Maudie's set had done that for the last coronation, and all they'd got for their pains was a stinking cold apiece. Along with thousands of others, they'd camped out on the pavement overnight and got soaked to the skin, and when the procession went by they'd hardly seen a thing because of the hordes of people in front of them. One of the girls had managed to drop her Brownie box camera, and someone had stepped on it, not even bothering to apologize, and that was the end of that.

3

The morning of Coronation Day did not start out well. Charlie declined to eat his breakfast, preferring instead to try to clamber out of his highchair, uttering cries of discontent. Maudie tried all the usual little tricks: a spoonful for Charlie and one for Mummy; puff puff, here comes the little puffer train — and down the little red tunnel we go! Nothing worked. Each time the spoon approached, he turned his head away.

'Shall I get the bacon started?' Dick called from the kitchen. 'Time's getting on.'

Maudie turned her head for a split second to answer him, and in that moment Charlie picked up his bowl and flung it on the floor, chortling with glee as it bounced away. Maudie gave a heavy sigh and called to Rover, who was delighted with the unexpected treat.

'I'd better make up a bottle,' she told

Dick, 'in case he kicks up a fuss later on.' Although of course he was on a diet of solid food now — when he deigned to eat it — Charlie still liked to have a bottle at times, especially when he was feeling out of sorts. It was best to be prepared for any eventuality.

In due course, the Bryants arrived at the manor house, looking forward to the day. Cora Beasley greeted them warmly and ushered them into her comfortable sitting room, where Harold Blunt and his wife Joan were already seated. The vicar rose to his feet as Maudie entered, followed by Dick, carrying their son.

'Doesn't Charlie look smart,' Joan enthused. 'What a handsome little fellow he is in that blue romper suit!' The handsome little fellow smiled at her. 'What a little angel he is with those golden curls. I suppose his hair may turn dark in time, don't you think?'

'If it does, it will match his temper,' Maudie muttered. 'He was certainly no angel when he woke up this morning!'

'Who else is coming?' Dick wondered, hoping to change the subject.

'My staff will be joining us; the indoor staff, that is. I didn't think it was fair to exclude them when the rest of us are watching the coronation under their own roof.' Mrs Beasley had both a cook and a housekeeper, which was a source of wonder to many people in the village, in these days when it was difficult to get staff. Since the war, women no longer wanted to go into domestic service; but rumour had it that the wealthy Cora Beasley paid well, and in any case, both of her helpers were childless widows who no doubt were glad of a comfortable home.

'And I've invited the new infants' teacher as well. I thought you'd like to meet her.'

Maudie was interested. 'So you've appointed a new one? I hadn't heard.'

'Yes, that's right. She's come to stay for a few days so Miss Probert can hand over the reins, so to speak, and she'll be taking up her duties in September.'

Maudie cast a look at the vicar. She would have loved to know what he was thinking, but his face was expressionless. Poor Gwyneth Probert had, in all innocence, stirred up a religious controversy at Christmas, and as a result had handed in her notice. Her contract stipulated that she must finish out the school year, but that was now coming to an end.

The young Welsh girl had a lovely soprano voice, and at Christmas she had been given a solo in the carol service at the church. The schoolchildren were part of this event because theirs was an Anglican church school.

Unfortunately, the church choir had an elderly member who had been performing solos for years, and she had been insulted at being passed over. People began to take sides, and one woman had even called at the school to berate the poor girl, saying that she had no right to sing in the church because she was Chapel. The vicar was caught in the middle of all this; and as for the timid Gwyneth, the furore was all too much. She was determined to go back to the valleys where she belonged.

Maudie turned to Joan Blunt. 'Have you met this new teacher? Do you think she'll fit in here?'

'Yes, we have. A no-nonsense sort of person, and some years older than Miss Probert. I expect she'll soon settle down, but the little ones adored Miss Probert and they'll be sad to see her go.'

The doorbell rang and Cora Beasley went to welcome the new arrival. 'This is Miss Verity Bourne, everyone. You've already met the vicar and Mrs Blunt, Miss Bourne. May I introduce Detective Sergeant and Mrs Bryant?'

Maudie looked at the newcomer with interest. Above-average height, dark hair cut in a fashionable bob, a determined jaw. Possibly in her mid-thirties. 'And this is our son, Charlie. I expect you'll be seeing him at school in three years' time, if you decide to stay.'

'Oh, I expect to be here for quite some time,' the woman said, holding out a slender hand and flashing a brilliant smile at Dick, who gave a sheepish grin in return.

So, it's like that, is it? Maudie thought. *I'll have to keep an eye on you, my girl. It seems to me you could be trouble, and that man is mine!* Rover seemed to have taken the measure of the new schoolmistress, for he bounded up to his master and pushed his nose between their clasped hands. 'And this is our dog, Rover,' Maudie continued.

Miss Bourne scowled at Rover. 'Actually, I don't much care for dogs. Dirty beasts. I'm surprised Mrs Beasley allows it in her lovely home.'

There was a crash of falling china. Maudie whirled round with a gasp of dismay to see a mixture of broken crockery and dismembered sandwiches, with Charlie sitting amidst the wreckage, clapping his hands in glee.

She knew at once what had happened. The refreshments had been set out on a pristine white tablecloth, and Charlie must have taken hold of it to help himself up. She had stopped using tablecloths at home for that very reason: a dangling cloth was an invitation to a curious young child.

Mrs Beasley bustled up, her face full of concern. Charlie offered her the broken handle of a tea cup. 'Handoo!' he announced, beaming.

'Thank you, darling. I'll take that now, shall I?' Mrs Beasley turned to Maudie. 'I'm so sorry, Nurse. I really should have thought when I brought out that oversized cloth. And you mustn't worry; this table only held the overflow. Most of the refreshments are on the big table by the window, along with the tea urn I borrowed from the W.I.'

Maudie's blood ran cold at the thought of what might have happened if Charlie had managed to tip scalding tea over his precious little body. Mortified beyond belief, she began to stammer apologies.

Verity Bourne's voice was quite audible over the hubbub. 'What a badly behaved child! Really, some people have no idea of proper parenting. I blame the mothers, of course. I see bad behaviour at school all the time, and poor mothering is always at the root of the trouble.'

As if to complete Maudie's humiliation, Rover began to nose among the wreckage, wolfing down meat paste sandwiches as he went.

Maudie wiped away a tear with the

back of her hand. 'We'll have to leave,' she whispered to Dick, who stood near the door with Charlie draped over his shoulder. 'It's all my fault! I only took my eyes off him for a second, and see what happened! How will we ever live this down?'

'Now, now, it's not the end of the world, old girl! Look, I'll take him home and keep him occupied, and you stay here and enjoy the coronation. I know how much you've been looking forward to it.'

Ever the gracious hostess, Cora Beasley assured them that no real harm had been done. 'Those weren't my favourite cups and saucers. I only decided to use them today because of their gold rims, which I thought appropriate for Coronation Day. They won't be missed, and I'm sure Mrs Banks will approve — a few less things to dust. Look, here she comes with a dustpan and brush, wearing a smile on her face!'

'You're very kind, Mrs Beasley, but I feel I can't stay, having cast such a dampener on the proceedings. Really, I cannot apologize enough.'

'Nonsense! Children will be children, and the main thing is that Charlie wasn't hurt. We shall all laugh about this in years to come, you can depend on that.'

'You're very kind, Mrs Beasley.'

Across the room, Joan Blunt patted the sofa beside her. 'Come and sit down, Nurse! This is what we've all been waiting for. The coronation is about to begin!'

4

Immersed in the historic events that were being shown on the tiny television screen, Maudie was able to forget her humiliation for a while. The watchers caught a glimpse of the great processions that preceded the Queen as she set out from Buckingham Palace on her way to the ancient Westminster Abbey where, just over five years earlier, she had married her fairy-tale prince.

At the west door, she was received by the archbishop and various bishops, and the great lords in the robes proclaiming them to be members of the ancient Orders of the Garter, the Thistle and the Bath.

The coronation regalia was carried in front of her as she walked, with her husband beside her, to the platform in the middle of the Abbey where she would be crowned. The commentator, speaking in a hushed voice, informed the watchers that the Archbishop of Canterbury, the Earl Marshal, and other dignitaries, would walk to all four sides of the platform to proclaim Elizabeth their queen. At the sound of trumpets, a mighty roar arose in the Abbey: 'God Save Queen Elizabeth!'

'God Save the Queen!' Mrs Beasley echoed.

There was, of course, much more to come; and, shamefully, Maudie found her mind wandering long before the crown was placed on the sovereign's head. What were the others thinking now? she wondered.

The Reverend Harold Blunt was no doubt following it all with greater understanding, being a man of the cloth; and of course, the Archbishop of Canterbury was the head of his Church, which gave them something in common.

When the camera focused briefly on the sad face of the late king's wife, now known as the Queen Mother, Cora Beasley probably felt a pang of recognition, being a widow herself. Maudie saw that little Prince Charles was sitting with his grandmother, solemnly taking it all in, although probably not understanding a great deal except that Mummy was the centre of the drama. The poor little chap was only four years old; surely they wouldn't expect him to sit through the whole thing? No, there was probably a nanny or someone waiting nearby, ready to whisk him away if he showed signs of flagging. Whatever happened, when he became monarch in his own right he would be able to say that he had witnessed his mother's coronation.

There was no sign of his little sister Anne. Very likely her parents had decided she was too young to stand the pace, and had wisely left her at home. If only Maudie had followed their example, she would not be branded as an incompetent mother now. Hindsight was indeed a wonderful thing!

For Maudie, the most emotional moment of the whole day came later. After the crown had been placed firmly on the Queen's head, Mrs Beasley's guests leapt to their feet as the music of the National Anthem burst forth, followed by the guns booming out from the Tower of London. When everyone was seated again, the Princes and Peers of the Realm came forward to declare homage to the Queen. First in line was her husband, and Maudie couldn't stop the tears flowing as she saw him kneel before his wife.

'I, Philip, Duke of Edinburgh, do become your liege man of life and limb and of earthly worship; and faith and truth I will bear unto you, to live and die, against all manner of folks. So help me God.'

To hear the man she loved say those words must mean the world to the young Queen, for didn't they echo the marriage vows the two of them had made to each other in 1947? And Maudie held fast to the belief that her Dick, although he would be embarrassed to admit in so many words, would similarly be ready to support and protect her all the days of their lives together, whatever the future might hold for them. And she made a solemn vow, there and then, that the pair of them would be the best possible parents to Charles Richard Bryant; so that some day, when he took his place in the world of grown-up men and women, he would be a man of honour and good repute.

★ ★ ★

'My goodness, that was wonderful!' Mrs Blunt exclaimed, standing up and stretching painfully after sitting for so long. 'But that poor girl must be absolutely exhausted after going through a day like that. And just imagine having the weight of that crown on her head. I wonder if she had the chance to practice wearing it before the big day?'

'And it's not over yet,' Cora Beasley said. 'What happens next, I wonder? Will she be able to go home and throw her shoes off, or slip into a nice hot bath?'

'Fat chance!' her cook said. 'They all have to appear on the balcony at the Palace, don't they? Let's hope someone gives her a cup of tea in her hand before she has to go and stand out on that balcony waving to all those thousands of people looking up at her.'

'And speaking of tea,' Mrs Beasley said,

'why don't we all have another cup? And do help yourselves to some of those finger sandwiches and fancies. I'm sure I don't want to be finishing them up all week.'

A short while later, Maudie was trudging down the long drive to the road, having turned down a drive home with the Blunts. This was partly because she needed to clear her head, but also because she had no wish to share the back seat of the car with Miss Bourne. It would be a long time before she could find it in her heart to excuse the unkind remarks the woman had made about Charlie, and her own parenting skills — or lack of them.

Yes, Charlie had been the cause of a regrettable accident — but he was not even two years old, and wasn't responsible. If it was anyone's fault, it was indeed Maudie's, for it had only been a matter of seconds for her to take her eyes off him, and chaos had ensued. But she hadn't been the only one present, so why hadn't anyone else noticed what was about to happen? Dick, for one; or Joan Blunt, who often babysat for them. On top of that, she wouldn't put it past that Verity to have seen Charlie heading for trouble, and done nothing.

The cottage was quiet when Maudie reached home. Dick was snoozing on the settee, and Charlie was nowhere in sight: presumably tucked up in his cot upstairs. Rover looked up from the rug when she entered, but for once he didn't thump his tail in greeting. Was no one going to welcome her home?

'Oh, hello,' Dick said, yawning. 'Did you have a nice time?'

'Very nice, thank you. And Mrs Beasley kindly sent you a plate of fancies.'

'That was nice of her.'

'You're not getting any meat paste sandwiches, though. Rover scoffed the lot.'

'Oh, yes, and he's been sick all over his basket in the scullery. I've left that for you to clean up: I've been busy with the boy, and haven't had time.'

'Thank you very much!'

She went upstairs to change out of her good clothes. She peeped into the nursery and spent a moment or two admiring the baby, sleeping like a little angel. Then it was downstairs to deal with Rover's mess while she waited for the kettle to boil for tea.

Dick was well away by the time she joined him, so she left him undisturbed. Kicking off her shoes, she sank into her own armchair and put her feet up on a footstool. It was good to be home!

Looking at her scrapbook would be a fitting end to the day, so she leafed through it, following the life of the pretty little girl who was now their Queen. She must watch out for suitable photos of the coronation in newspapers and magazines. Mrs Hatch at the shop knew of her interest and would probably have something suitable put by.

There was one photo that never failed to tug at her heartstrings. It was called 'The Three Queens', and it showed three heavily veiled women mourning the late King as they arrived for his funeral last year. Queen Mary, his old mother who had not lived to see her granddaughter crowned because she had died only a few weeks ago; Elizabeth, his wife, too young to be a widow at fifty-one; and his daughter, Elizabeth, who had been crowned today. Maudie had never met any one of them, but to her they felt like family, and today she had seen one of that family set forth to fulfil her destiny. It was a good feeling.

5

A chastened Maudie sat in the vicarage garden, sipping coffee. Charlie, wearing a cotton sunhat, sat in his pushchair, happily watching Rover frolicking with Perkin, the vicarage cat. After months of animosity, the two animals had at last come to terms with each other, although Perkin wasn't above giving Rover a slap with a heavy paw if he got too close.

'I thought I'd stroll up to the manor house this afternoon and grovel to Cora Beasley,' Maudie said. 'After yesterday's little episode, I really feel I should.'

'I'm sure there's no need for that,' Joan Blunt murmured. 'She's fond of them both, and I'm sure she understands.'

'I know, but still . . . '

'You could always write a letter, or choose a pretty card.'

'No, my mind is made up. The thing is, I'd like to take a small gift as a peace offering, but I can't decide what. I thought of a bunch of pretty flowers from the garden, but I'm afraid that would only be a case of coals to Newcastle. She already has that fantastic perennial border, not to mention that little patch of flowers kept especially for cutting. Dick suggested taking her some of his vegetables. Isn't that just like a man?'

'He's proud of his marrows,' Joan said, smiling.

'I know, but the same thing applies! She has a full-time gardener to grow anything she could ever wish for, not to mention a greenhouse with tomatoes and cucumbers galore!'

'Cora Beasley is very fond of Turkish delight, and I happen to know that Mrs Hatch took delivery of a new batch of sweets yesterday. I'm sure I saw her putting some round boxes up on the shelf where little fingers can't get hold of them.'

'Turkish Delight, eh? That's not something I'd like to receive, but if you're sure . . . '

'Absolutely! And now that sweets have come off the ration at last, she'll be able to indulge her sweet tooth.'

Maudie looked down at her feet. 'I'm rather dreading going up there. I've never been so humiliated in all my life. Oh, I know she was very gracious and said it didn't matter, but I just didn't know where to look! And if Dick hadn't come to the rescue, I'd have had to leave, and I'd have missed seeing the coronation!'

'As Mrs Beasley so rightly said, some day we'll look back on this and laugh. Can't you look at it in that light, Nurse? I know it was a bit awkward for you, but Charlie is still a baby, and these things do happen.'

'Charlie may be innocent, but what does it say about me? Am I a feckless mother? I'm a midwife, Mrs Blunt! When I think back at all the advice I've given to new mothers on how to cope, it makes me feel ashamed. Why can't I practise what I preach?'

Her friend laughed. 'There is nothing wrong with your mothering skills, Nurse! If you're fretting about what Miss Bourne said, don't give it another thought. That young woman is far too outspoken, and

I'm afraid I foresee trouble ahead once she becomes part of our community. Another cup of coffee?'

* * *

July came, when Charlie Bryant was to celebrate his second birthday. 'I suppose we'll be in for trouble now the Terrible Twos are officially here,' Dick said. 'Are we going to give him a birthday party?'

'I think he's a bit young for it. Shall we give him another year before we get involved with all that?'

Maudie had sometimes been invited to parties given for the children she had brought into the world, and had experienced her share of chaos. Little girls who wet their knickers because of all the excitement. Little boys who became too rough during the party games, as little boys would. Musical chairs has a lot to answer for! Jelly and blancmange and chocolate cake trodden into the carpet. She could write a book!

'I might invite Mrs Blunt over for a cup of tea on the day. She is his godmother, after all. But then we should ask the godfather as well. I don't suppose Bill Brewer would be free to come?'

'He's going to be away on a course that week. Why don't you ask Cora Beasley to make up the numbers? She can tip the table over and mash the birthday cake to bits. Give her the chance to get her own back.'

'Oh, do shut up, Dick Bryant!'

'Just a thought.'

'No, I don't think I will ask her. She'd only feel she had to bring him something, and I don't want that. I once heard her say that because she's wealthy she gets invited to all the christenings and weddings in the parish, even when she doesn't know the people from Adam. People hoping to get a nice present, you see.'

'Oh, I'm sure it can't be that bad, old girl!'

'It's this lady of the manor thing, Dick. She's supposed to go around patting children's heads and doling out six-pences. It's expected of her.'

'Do you really think so? A lot of things

have changed since the war.'

'Not all that much.' The trouble was that Cora Beasley wasn't part of the gentry: neither fish nor fowl nor good red herring. Her late husband, a wealthy businessman, had bought the Manor House from its aristocratic owner, whose family name would die with him because his three sons had perished in the Great War. The local response to this was divided between resentment of the newcomers, and the expectation that everything would continue as before, with a kindly landlord at the helm.

Widowed now, Cora Beasley found herself automatically considered for every position and privilege having to do with village life. Head of the Mothers' Union, a governor of the school, provider of employment, and godmother to numerous babies. *Noblesse oblige*, she'd been heard to say, laughing.

The big day came. Joan Blunt arrived, carrying a small parcel. Dick managed to get home from work in time to take a photo of his son blowing out the candles on his birthday cake — which he did, with a little help from his mother.

Dick had bought a fairy cycle for the baby: a small, very basic vehicle that in due course would be replaced by a proper tricycle. Eager to show the child how to operate it, he sat Charlie down on its wooden seat — only to have him scramble off at once. Disappointed, Dick scooped him up and tried again. The two women watched in amusement as Charlie smacked his father's hand and got down on the floor in a hurry.

'If at first you don't succeed . . . ' Once more, Dick tried to initiate his son into the mysteries of the wheel. Frustrated, Charlie set up a howl that made Joan Blunt clap her hands over her ears.

'Sorry!' Maudie mouthed, unheard over the din. 'That's enough of that, young man!' She deposited the struggling child in his highchair and thrust a chocolate biscuit into his little paw. The noise stopped abruptly.

'Sorry!' Joan said. 'I didn't mean to criticize. I was a bit startled for a minute, that's all.'

'Chocky bick!' Charlie mumbled, through

a mouthful of crumbs.

'Bribery and corruption!' Dick said.

'You're just upset because he wouldn't cooperate with his fairy cycle. He'll love it when he gets used to it, I promise you. Meanwhile, why don't you blow up this? It should keep him occupied for a bit and help him forget about the you-know-what.' Maudie handed Dick a blue balloon.

Joan Blunt had given Charlie a squeaky toy in the form of a green rubber frog. After a few false starts, during which he held it upside down and tried to bite the nose off the creature, he got the hang of things and squeezed it with both hands, squealing every time it squeaked.

'Thank you very much, Mrs Blunt! Maybe you can bring him a set of drums next year!' Maudie moaned, but she was smiling as she said it.

★ ★ ★

In the days that followed, Charlie did indeed take a liking to his fairy cycle, although Maudie rued the day that her

44

husband had bought it. The lawn wasn't the best place for it because the solid rubber wheels got stuck in the turf, and naturally they couldn't let their toddler use it outside on the road. That only left the house, and Charlie spent many happy moments scooting himself around the sitting room, bashing table legs, and getting stuck behind the settee before having to be rescued by his long-suffering parents.

After a few painful collisions, poor Rover learned to get out of the way when the juggernaut approached, and even Maudie suffered from barked shins at times.

'I'm glad that uppity Miss Bourne can't see this carry-on,' she muttered as she replaced a pile of magazines that had fallen from an overturned basket. 'I can't think what she'd have to say about it!'

And so life went on, as one happy summer day succeeded another, and small Charlie Bryant went from strength to strength.

6

September came, with an air of purpose-fulness. Children returned to school, greeting their friends with wild delight, and the strident tones of the school bell once again penetrated the consciousness of nearby residents. Many of the young-sters had new shoes; seeing this, Maudie observed that better times had at last reached England. During the war, when the slogan had been Make Do and Mend, so many children had gone to school in hand-me-downs and down-at-heel shoes because replacements simply were not available in the shops.

But then, we were all shabby in those days, she recalled. The only well-dressed women had been those in the services, who wore uniforms. The colours might be drab, the skirts ill-cut, but at least everything matched.

Maudie and Dick hadn't been away for a summer holiday. 'Perhaps next year,'

Dick had said after Charlie's birthday. 'Things are a bit tight at the moment. I sometimes wonder if we were wrong to take on this mortgage. Do you ever regret it, Maudie?'

'Not for a minute. This has been my home for so long, it would have broken my heart to leave it.' The cottage had come with the job when Maudie had been the midwife for the Llandyfan district, even before she'd met Dick. Much had changed with the introduction of the new National Health Service, and shortly after their marriage, the cottage had come up for sale by the local council, whose property it was. After much soul-searching, the couple had put in an offer, which was accepted.

'I must admit, I'd love to take the boy on a seaside holiday,' Dick went on. 'I used to envy my chums who were lucky enough to have treats like that. They'd come back full of stories about making sand castles, or having boat trips, or riding the scenic railway at a funfair. Of course, there was nothing like that for me. Poor Mum had enough of a struggle to put meals on the table without ever dreaming about a holiday. I tell you, Maudie, when we do go away I shall have as much fun as the boy, making up for lost time. I shall buy a bucket and spade and build the biggest castle anyone has ever seen. Rover will help me dig a moat, and you can fill it with seawater. I'll put a flag on top . . . '

Maudie smiled. 'And then Charlie will jump on your castle and bring it tumbling down.'

'Bliss!' said her husband.

★　★　★

The bustle of activity around the village left Maudie feeling vaguely dissatisfied, as she confided to Mrs Blunt. 'Am I being ungrateful?' she asked her friend. 'I know I have everything to be thankful for: a lovely home, a kind husband, a dear little boy. Yet a little voice in my head seems to keep asking, 'Is this all there is?' Am I going to spend the rest of my life mopping up after Dick and Charlie, with the highlight of my day being watching for Dick to come in the door after work, and putting his tea down in front of him? Of course I'd be devastated — gutted — if anything happened to either one of them, but it does seem as if there should be more to life than this!'

'You're missing your work, I'm sure. All these years as a nurse and midwife meant a great deal to you.'

'Indeed they did; although on blustery mornings when I was forced to cycle around the district, soaked to the skin, I'd have given anything to be able to stay at home while my husband went out to bring home the bacon!'

Joan laughed. 'That's human beings for you. Never satisfied! But surely there's something you can do? I know that married women can't nurse full-time, but I wonder if there isn't a compromise somehow. Could you get a day's work just now and then, perhaps filling in when the District Nurse falls ill? Or doing a couple of hours a day in some medically-related work, such as receptionist-cum-chaperone in the doctor's surgery?'

'Funnily enough, I did suggest something similar to Dick. Oh, not rushing into anything right away; just seeing what might be available.'

'And?'

'And he couldn't put his foot down fast enough. Of course, he has a point. I'd have to get someone to look after Charlie, and anything I could earn would be wiped out by what I had to pay her.'

'But perhaps if you pointed out that the stimulation of a little job would leave you feeling brighter, more satisfied with your lot . . . ?'

'It's no good. Something about his income tax, and how we'd be worse off in the end after we'd done our sums.'

★ ★ ★

Maudie went to the village shop in search of cinnamon. Both Dick and Charlie had developed a taste for cinnamon toast, where you spread brown sugar on thickly-buttered toast, then shook powdered cinnamon on top. It probably wasn't good for either of them, but such treats had been unavailable for so long during sugar rationing that she didn't have the heart to deny her

50

husband what he craved.

The baby, of course, wanted what he saw Daddy eating, and although Maudie had tried to improve matters by hiding a layer of stewed prunes under the sugar, he had quickly discovered the ploy and dropped his toast on the floor with a shout of disgust. Rover hadn't fancied it, either.

At the shop, she found Mrs Hatch deep in conversation with a woman who obviously had a grievance. Heads together, they were muttering darkly about what they might do if something happened again.

'Good morning, Nurse Bryant. I'll be with you shortly. Do you know Mrs Polley? She lives up the prefabs. Perhaps Nurse can tell you what you ought to do, dear.'

'How do you do, Mrs Polley? Can I help? Is anyone ill?'

'Not to say ill, but it's my poor little grandson, Eddie. You should just see his poor little hands!'

'It's that new schoolmistress, Miss Bourne!' Mrs Hatch explained. 'She's given little Eddie the cane. A great slash across each the palm of each hand: I saw them with my own eyes. The poor little chap is five years old, Nurse. Only started school this week. Why, it's enough to put him off book learning for life.'

'She'll cop it good and proper when his dad comes back from sea. Expected home any day now, he is, and he's got a temper on him like you wouldn't believe. Nate Lunney can flare up quicker than a tissue paper on a bonfire.

'I won't say I'm against punishing them as does wrong,' Mrs Polley went on. 'Spare the rod and spoil the child: that's what it says in the Bible. And when I was at school, you got a taste of the cane right enough, and it did us no harm. In fact, you got another licking if you went home and complained. My dad used to say we must've done something to deserve it. But what could a kiddie the size of our Eddie have done? I ask you!'

'They've made a mistake, taking on the likes of her!' Mrs Hatch said, nodding. 'What do we know about the woman? She's supposed to have come from up north somewhere, but why did she come all the way down here unless she's got something to hide?'

'Do you have any cinnamon, Mrs Hatch?' Maudie was anxious to be gone. She'd been holding Charlie on her hip since entering the shop, and now he was struggling to get down. If she stood him on his feet, he'd be off in a flash, creating mayhem.

'Yes, it's on that shelf with the mustard and that. But before you go, isn't there something you can do to help Mrs Polley and their Eddie?'

'I'm sorry, I really don't have anything to do with the school now I'm no longer nursing. Surely it's up to the parents to make a complaint?'

'Huh!' Mrs Polley said. 'Never mind what I said before, I doubt you could drag that dad of his out of the Spread Eagle long enough to say boo to a goose when he does come home. And our Edith could never summon up the nerve to go and speak to a teacher. She only went to school until Standard Six, and that's more schooling than I ever had. No, it needs somebody who's had a bit of education, see. If you'd go and have a word with Miss Bourne, I'd be that grateful, and so would his ma.'

'Nurse Bryant here could face a dragon in its den!' Mrs Hatch announced. 'She's faced murderers on the rampage, she has, and lived to tell the tale; haven't you, Nurse?'

While Maudie couldn't help relishing the compliment, she was none too pleased at being manipulated like this. She had only come here to buy a jar of cinnamon, and see where it had landed her! She was now committed to tackling the bossy Miss Bourne, about something that was really none of her business.

'I suppose I could try,' she said weakly.

7

In the cool of the evening, the Bryants went for a walk down the road. Because few of the local people possessed cars, the road was usually deserted at this time of day, so Dick had brought Charlie's fairy cycle along, assuring Maudie that he would keep the child out of harm's way. For a little while, the boy trundled along manfully in Rover's wake, scuffing his shoes in the process, but then he got tired of the effort and demanded to be picked up.

Now he was riding piggyback on Dick's shoulders, and Maudie was lumbered with the toy. She had tried leaving it in the ditch, as they would be coming back this way very shortly, but Charlie set up such a fuss when he saw his beloved cycle being cast aside that she was forced to retrieve it and carry it with her.

A figure loomed in the distance. Obviously they were not the only ones taking the evening air. With a feeling of doom, Maudie recognized the oncoming pedestrian as the charming Verity Bourne. What was worse, she hadn't yet summoned up the courage to tackle the woman about her treatment of little Eddie, and dared not pop into the shop again until she had done it. The problem was that Miss Bourne would be quite justified in saying that Maudie had no business interfering in the life of the school. She wasn't a parent. She didn't even know the little boy in question.

Their paths met. Miss Bourne spoke first. 'Good evening, Dick! Lovely evening, isn't it?'

Maudie bridled. Well! Since when had those two been on first-name terms?

'Good evening, Miss Bourne,' Dick answered. 'Yes, it is. Out for a walk, are you?'

Well, she's not flying her kite! Maudie thought. Would the woman deign to acknowledge her? Apparently not, for she smiled up at Dick as if they were two old friends.

'You have your little boy out with you, I

see. It must have been so disappointing for you to miss the coronation, and quite noble of you to take charge of the child when his mother couldn't manage him.'

'Oh, I listened in on the wireless for a bit; and of course there was a lot in the newspapers at the time. I'm not one for all these social occasions among the teacups, you know. I was quite happy to pig it at home in my old gardening togs.'

'Even so, it was foolish of your wife to bring him to the manor house on such an auspicious occasion. And as for that smelly dog of hers . . . '

Maudie controlled her temper with great difficulty. *Give the awful woman enough rope, and she might hang herself,* she thought.

Not as easily upset, Dick gave a forced laugh and murmured something about Cora Beasley being fond of Charlie and Rover, so she had issued a special invitation to both of them, however ill-advised that had turned out to be.

'Yes, I see; and I'm sure this little fellow will be quite sweet when he's learned how to behave in polite company. If you like, I can give you some tips on how to handle him. I am rather an expert in these matters, you know.'

'Thank you, Miss Bourne. I'll bear that in mind. And now we really must carry on if we're to get Charlie home before his bedtime.' Dick moved on, followed by Rover, leaving Maudie standing alone. The school teacher hesitated, as if she meant to give up her own walk and follow Dick.

Right! That does it, lady! Maudie girded herself for battle. 'Excuse me!'

Miss Bourne turned, raising one eyebrow. An eyebrow in dire need of plucking, Maudie noted. 'Yes? What is it, Mrs Bryant?'

'Oh, so you do know my name, then?'

'I don't know what you mean.'

'I think you do, Miss Bourne, and I'll thank you to keep your opinions of my son's behaviour to yourself.'

'Every child needs discipline, Mrs Bryant. If he doesn't receive it in a timely manner, those in authority over him are simply storing up trouble for the future.'

'And I suppose you were only avoiding

58

future trouble when you thrashed that poor little boy who is unlucky enough to be a member of your class!'

'I don't know what you're talking about.'

'A little boy called Eddie. I met his grandmother the other day. She was greatly distressed because the child came home with bright red marks on both hands, having been caned by you!'

'And did this woman tell you why I had to punish the boy?'

'No, but surely a five-year-old — a newcomer to school life, at that — can't have done anything so bad as to get the cane!'

Miss Bourne heaved a sigh. Speaking slowly, as to a not-very-bright pupil, she explained what had occurred. 'Eddie is a big boy for his age and a bully with it. He hasn't learned to share, and if he doesn't get his own way, he gets rough. He pushed a little girl off her chair on the first day of term because he wanted her blue Plasticine and he'd been given red. He deliberately broke another child's crayons, for no other reason than pure spite, as far as I could tell.'

'So you caned him!'

'Not at once, no. At first, I took him aside and appealed to his better nature. When that didn't work, I made him stand in the corner, except that he wouldn't remain there and he started roaming around the room, disrupting the class. I only ran out of patience when he bit another child on the arm because the boy wouldn't hand over the apple he brought for his playtime snack. I really couldn't allow that, Mrs Bryant; so, yes, I gave him a dose of his own medicine.'

This put a different complexion on the affair, although Maudie still felt that the punishment meted out was far too severe. Now she was stuck with justifying the teacher's behaviour — at least, up to a point — which would leave her as piggy-in-the-middle. She would have to do her best to avoid bumping into Grandma Polley again.

'Now, if you've quite finished quizzing me on my teaching methods, Mrs Bryant, I must be on my way. I don't have time to continue my walk now that you've kept me talking. I have tomorrow's lessons to prepare. Goodbye!' She turned away and hurried in the direction taken by Dick.

Maudie became aware that she was still holding Charlie's fairy cycle by the bar that served as a backrest. How satisfactory it would be to swing it in a wide arc and feel it make contact with this insufferable woman's skull! It was such a pity that they lived in a so-called civilised society. 'If somebody doesn't strangle that woman before she's very much older, I'll eat my hat!' she muttered.

Rover came running up to Maudie, wearing a soppy grin on his face. A terrible odour reached her nostrils.

'Oh, no! What have you done, you wretched dog?' She knew only too well. His greatest delight was to roll in something disgusting, usually some such article as a squirrel or a rabbit that had been dead for some time. What on earth was that all about? Only a dog knew the answer to that, and Rover couldn't talk.

'You know what this means, don't you, old boy? Bathtime!' His tail drooped and he whined sadly. 'If you were any kind of dog, you'd chase after that Verity Bourne and jump up on her nice clean skirt, but sadly you're too well-behaved.'

Narrowing her eyes against the sun, Maudie was just able to see, far down the road, her Dick and Verity Bourne strolling together, side by side. If she hurried, she could still catch up with them, but why should she? She wouldn't give the hussy the satisfaction.

'Come on, Rover, home we go! And I don't think I'll bother giving you a bath at all. That's a treat in store for Dick Bryant. My time will be taken up with putting Charlie to bed. I can't be expected to do everything.'

Perhaps it was unfair of Maudie to take it out on Dick — but did he have to be so polite to the schoolteacher? Surely he owed something to his wife when Verity was so obviously baiting her?

In her mind, she harked back to the words that had almost reduced her to tears during the coronation ceremony. 'I am your liege man of life and limb and of earthly worship; and faith and truth I will bear unto you, to live and die, against all manner of folks.' Maudie was willing to bet that the handsome Duke of Edinburgh would make short work of the likes of Miss Verity Bourne!

8

Emerging from church on a bright September morning, Maudie was greeted by Dora Frost, wife of the landlord of the Spread Eagle. 'You don't have your little boy with you this morning, I see.'

'No, he was a bit fussy in the night, so I've left him at home with Dick.'

'Ah! You have a real treasure in that hubby of yours! It's not every man who would have put up with having a kiddie foisted on him on his day off.'

Maudie swallowed a rude retort. She had fought this battle throughout her career as a midwife, and it wasn't won yet. Why shouldn't a man help to take care of his young child? Why did so many chaps still feel it wasn't manly to be seen in public, pushing a pram? Still, she knew that Dora didn't mean anything by it, so she managed a smile and agreed that Dick was indeed one in a thousand.

'I've been wanting to speak to you,'

Mrs Frost went on, 'because there was a chap asking for you last week. Said he knew you in the old days, whatever that means.'

'Oh, yes?' It was probably the husband of one of her former patients whose child she had delivered. She was always running into old acquaintances, having a struggle to recall the men's names, although she never forgot a mother or a baby.

'He's a rep for one of the big stationery companies. Actually, he was a bit shabby, down-at-heel, so I was a bit wary about giving out information, in case you didn't want to get involved. But then I thought: well, if I don't say where you live, somebody else will, on account of everyone hereabouts knowing everything about you. And if he does turn out to be an awkward customer, you'll be safe as houses with a bobby for a husband.'

Maudie was intrigued. 'Is he staying with you now?'

'No, he went on his way this morning, but he says he'll be passing through again next week and he'll look you up then.'

'Did he happen to give you his name?'

'Of course, when he registered. My Len is ever so strict about that, on account of the income tax for thing, and in case the police ever want to ask questions, for another. You know how we've had some pretty dodgy customers staying in the past: killers and that!'

Maude did. 'And his name is?'

'Oops! Didn't I say? I'd forget my head if it wasn't screwed on. Gerald Saunders. Jerry, he said to call him. Does that ring any bells?'

Maudie had to think. Jerry Saunders? 'Could it be possible?' she murmured.

'You know him, then, Nurse? An old flame, is it?'

'No, no, nothing like that. A chap of that name lived next door to us when I was a girl. We went to the same school, although he left before I did. The last I heard of him, he'd been called up into the Army, but I don't know what became of him after that.'

'Ah, it'll be nice for you both to have a bit of a natter, then. Catch up on old times.'

* ★ ★

Maudie arrived home to a rapturous welcome from Rover, and a grunt from Dick, who was immersed in the Sunday papers.

'I'm home! Is Charlie all right?'

'Haven't heard a peep from him all the while you've been gone.'

'I'll just dash up and have a look, then.' Charlie was probably asleep, yet Maudie knew that long silences could be ominous where two-year-olds were concerned. He might have learned to climb over the side of his cot while she was gone, and could even now be redecorating the upstairs with her lipsticks, if not something far worse. On this occasion, however, all was well. He was sound asleep with his thumb in his mouth, looking like a Botticelli angel.

'Everything all right?' Dick looked up as she tiptoed down the stairs.

'All quiet on the Western Front.'

'Good-oh! Pop the kettle on, will you, love? I'm parched.'

Having checked to make sure that all was well with their Sunday dinner, which she had put on to cook before leaving for church, Maudie made tea and rejoined her husband.

'I saw Dora Frost after the service,' she began.

'Oh, yes? What did she have to say?'

'Apparently they've had someone staying — one of the reps they put up — and he thinks he knows me.'

'And who is this bloke?'

'His name is Jerry Saunders, and I think he might be an old neighbour of ours, from when I was a schoolgirl. If it is him, it's a real face from the past.'

'And you haven't see him since?'

'No. You know how it was in the war. People got separated. Jerry got called up; his family got bombed out in the Blitz like mine did; and I was already away from home nursing.'

'So what does he want with you now?'

Maudie shrugged. 'Perhaps he just wants to chat about old times. Come to think of it, I don't even know how he tracked me down. Dora didn't say.'

'So, what do you expect me to do about it? You won't be inviting him to stay here, I hope?'

'Hardly. For one thing, we don't have the accommodation, with Charlie occupying what used to be the spare room. Besides, they have plenty of space at the pub. I might invite him to tea, though, if that's all right with you. You wouldn't mind, would you?'

'Of course I wouldn't mind, love. In fact, I'll even be here when he comes, if that's what you want.'

'We'll see. For all I know, he may not even follow through.'

Dick was no longer listening. He continued to turn the pages of his newspaper, paying particular attention to the sports articles. At least he didn't feel threatened by an unknown man coming to look up his wife out of the blue!

Maudie, busy in the kitchen, wondered if Jerry would look any different today from the gangly, sandy-haired youth who had been known as 'Carrots' at school. What had his life been like in the intervening years? Was he married? He might even be the father of grown-up children by now. What would he think of her after all these years, happily settled with a husband and a toddler, a lengthy and successful career behind her?

The smell of roast beef wafted through the house as Maudie made the gravy. It would be lovely if she and Dick could enjoy a quiet meal together before Charlie woke up. Such occasions were few and far between nowadays; but if their son joined them, she would keep him quiet with a bit of Yorkshire pudding to chew on while they ate, and feed him properly later when Dick had gone out to survey his garden. They were having peas and carrots today, and she could do without the sight of the baby squashing peas in his chubby little hands, or using carrots as missiles to attack Rover.

'Something smells good! What's for afters?' Dick asked, coming into the kitchen and planting a kiss on the back of Maudie's neck as she bent over the oven.

'Stewed apple.'

'Aw! I was hoping for jam roly-poly with lashings of custard.'

'Not on top of a good roast dinner, Dick. The combination is far too heavy. It would sit on your stomach all afternoon, and the next thing you knew, you'd be reaching for the bicarb.'

What Maudie was kind enough to keep to herself was the fact that Dick was beginning to put on weight, and if he didn't watch out he'd begin to resemble a roly-poly pudding himself. She had already let out the waist of his everyday trousers once this year, and she knew for a fact that he needed to undo the top buttons of his gardening trousers when he bent over to harvest his vegetables.

If she really cared about her husband, she would stand firm and serve more suitable foods, such as the salads he detested, and desserts like junket or fruit. But what was the point of that? He'd only thwart her by overindulging in the police canteen.

And, she thought, *let's face it; who am I to talk?* Her smart red dress with the white spots was too tight over the bosom, so that it gaped a bit when she tried to fasten the buttons. She'd already moved them over once, and that was all she could do. It was a pity, really, as it was one of her favourite summer frocks. For now, she would leave it hanging in the wardrobe, in the hope that it would still be in fashion by the time she had managed to shed that unwanted five pounds. (*Or ten pounds*, the wicked imp on her shoulder whispered in her ear.)

9

Maudie woke up with a shock, shaking from a nightmare in which a faceless horror was chasing her, intent on snatching little Charlie from her arms. She lay still, trying to slow her racing heart. The alarm clock on the bedside table said a quarter past three. Beside her, Dick snored softly. There was no sound from the baby's room.

It was no surprise that she should have the occasional nightmare, for just before last Christmas, Charlie had been kidnapped. Actually, he had only been missing for a short while before the faithful Rover had found him, lying safe and sound in the manger in the outdoor nativity display at the church; but she would never forget those agonizing moments when she discovered her child missing.

Go to sleep, Maudie! Charlie is safe in his cot, and morning will come all too soon! But, try as she might, she was unable to nod off again. To distract herself, she let her mind travel back down the years to the days when she was a girl, and poor Jerry Saunders her faithful swain.

Swain! That was Grandma's word, as old-fashioned as the woman herself. Jerry was her best friend's grandson, and the children had been thrown together since early childhood, with dark hints about the possibility of the two families being linked together by marriage in due course.

Grandma had come to live with Maudie's family in their terraced house after her husband died. It was a bit of a squash with only two bedrooms: Maudie and her sister Minnie shared a bed in a curtained-off section of what was now Grandma's retreat. It wasn't ideal, but in those days people looked after their own.

Maudie had just started at the council school round the corner when Dad disappeared. 'He's gone away to war, love, to be a soldier. We must all be very brave and make him proud. He'll soon come back to us all. They say it will all be over by Christmas, and then you'll see him marching up the street, and you'll run and give him a big kiss, won't you?'

But it wasn't over by Christmas. Maudie watched and waited, but Dad didn't come. Then, one day, Jerry came to school with tears running down his face. Maudie was deeply shocked, for Jerry was older than her, a big boy in Standard Three, and big boys didn't blub! Hearing the other boys jeering at Jerry, the headmaster called the school to order.

'Saunders has had bad news, children. His father has been killed at the Front. He has died a glorious death, giving his life for king and country.'

Jerry bucked up a bit after hearing that, but now Maudie had a new worry. What if she never saw Dad again? How could she bear it?

One day she came back from school, complaining of being hungry, which was nothing new. Shouting, 'Is there any bread and jam?' she came to a halt in the kitchen, where her mother and Grandma were oblivious to her arrival.

'Thank God! Oh, thank God!' her mother kept saying, over and over.

'What is it? What's happened?' Maudie felt she'd burst if somebody didn't explain what was going on.

'It's your dad, love,' Grandma said. 'He's been wounded, at the war.'

'Why is Mum happy if he's hurt?'

'Because he'll be coming home now, and the beastly Hun won't be able to get at him and kill him dead.'

'Oh. But won't he get better, like I did when I sprained my ankle? Won't they make him go back and fight some more?'

'No chance of that. He's lost a leg. Heaven knows what's to become of us all now.' Grandma sighed.

Four-year-old Minnie couldn't understand. 'Why has he lost it, Maudie? Can't he go back and look for it?'

'No, you silly-billy. Do you want to come and play hopscotch? I've got a new stone. It slides ever so well.'

Jerry had had to leave school as soon as the inspector would let him. He was the man of the house now, and had to help support his ma and sisters. He found a job as a delivery boy for the grocer's shop, spending long days furiously pedalling a boneshaker bicycle, taking supplies to the homes of the well-to-do.

'Do you want to come for a walk or something after church on Sunday?' he asked Maudie, twisting his cap in his hands until it resembled a rag.

'I s'pose I might,' she told him. His face flushed with pleasure.

Walking out with a boy meant something. After months or even years of that, a chap would take the girl home to meet his mother; and if she passed that test, the next step would be an engagement. That, too, might drag on for years until the couple could save up enough money to get married. All too often a life of poverty followed, with numerous children to support.

Maudie wasn't worried. Mrs Saunders had known her since she was born, and it was clear that she already approved of the future union. She even went so far as to suggest they could start married life in her front bedroom. At fourteen, Maudie wasn't looking that far ahead. She had a boyfriend, and that was all that mattered.

The headmaster paid a call on

Maudie's parents. He found her father in their living room, busily cutting up second-hand clothes they had found at the market. His wife, who was clever with the needle, would wash and press the pieces and remake them into something saleable. The income would supplement his meagre pension.

'Maudie is a bright girl,' Mr James began, when the ritual pleasantries had been exchanged. 'I would like to see her get the chance to improve herself. Will you consider letting her train as a pupil teacher? She will teach the younger children by day, and attend night classes in the town once a week.'

'Oh, no,' Maudie's mother said. 'It's very kind of you to think of our Maudie, but she's already spoken for. She has a job waiting for her at the greengrocer's and we need the money.'

The headmaster knew when he was beaten. Maudie didn't know whether to be disappointed or not. She was more concerned as to when Jerry might summon up the courage to kiss her. When he did it would be a red-letter day, but she was half-dreading that she might get it wrong. Where did you put the noses? Wouldn't they get in the way when you tried to get your lips together?

When the big moment finally arrived it was a crushing disappointment. Jerry planted a wet kiss on Maudie's trembling lips and stood back, full of himself. 'You want a pen'orth of chips?' he asked.

'Might as well,' Maudie muttered. 'Make sure you put plenty of salt and vinegar on them.'

★   ★   ★

Minnie was fourteen when she died. For some time she had been suffering with a mysterious pain in her side, but her parents had put off taking her to a doctor because doctors cost money. Finally, when it could no longer be put off, she was admitted to hospital, where doctors tried to save her. By then it was too late, for the appendix had 'blown up and burst' as Grandma told anyone who would listen.

Maudie, putting parsnips and winter

cabbages on display outside the shop, looked at her numb and reddened hands, and made a decision. 'I'm going in for nursing,' she told her parents. 'Don't try to talk me out of it. If we'd known what might happen we could have saved Minnie. We'd have found the money somewhere, you know we would.'

Too stunned to argue, Dad gave permission. Maudie applied to a big hospital where they trained girls who wanted to nurse, and was accepted. Now her relationship with Jerry was the only barrier to her ambitions.

'I'm so sorry, Jerry, but it never would have worked. We're two very different people. We want different things out of life.'

'I'll wait for you, Maudie,' he pleaded. 'Three years isn't long. Plenty of people have longer engagements than that.'

'But they don't let married women work in hospitals, Jerry. What would be the point of going through all that for nothing?'

He tried to change her mind, of course, but in the end there was nothing he could say or do. Maudie left the little terraced house and never looked back.

'And that's what I shouldn't be doing now,' she murmured.

Dick rolled over onto her side of the bed. 'Wassat?'

'Nothing, dear. Go back to sleep.'

And moments later she, too, was asleep again.

10

'Who was that on the phone?' Dick looked up from his magazine as Maudie came in from the hall.

'Cora Beasley, with an invitation to tea this afternoon.'

He groaned. 'Do we have to? I was hoping to put in some time on the garden this afternoon. This is the weekend, you know. The only time I get off.'

'Keep your hair on. It doesn't include you.'

'What about Charlie, then? Do you expect him to nap all afternoon?'

'You can have him outside with you, can't you?'

'I suppose so, but it's not very convenient. Do you have to come running every time she beckons?'

'That's hardly fair, Dick. And after that Coronation business I feel I have to show a bit of give and take. And you know that Charlie will be safe enough outside with you now you've fenced in the garden. Make sure the gate is firmly latched and he'll amuse himself quite happily while you work.'

'That's all very well, Maudie, but what if he has a fall, or needs his nappy changed? How am I supposed to deal with that with mud all over my hands?'

'Oh, very well, you old grouch! I'll call her back and say I can't make it.'

'No need for that, old girl. I was only saying.'

Dick seemed to have been saying a great deal lately. Every time they set foot outside the door they seemed to stumble across that Miss Bourne, who made for Dick like a homing pigeon thankful to reach the safety of the loft. She was either praising him for being such a forbearing husband, or commiserating with him for being stuck with such a poor wife as Maudie. Not that she said so in so many words! She was far too clever for that, but there was no doubt in Maudie's mind that the beastly woman was out to snare Dick!

'Do you want me to run you up to the

Manor house?' Dick asked.

'No, thanks. I'll take the bike.'

'You haven't ridden the bike since you gave up the job.'

'Then perhaps it's time I took it up again.' Cycling was just the way to lose a few of those unwanted pounds. The trouble with motherhood was that you couldn't stride out purposefully when you went shopping or somewhere because you had to match your stride to that of a two year old, or hang on to a pram.

Soon she was speeding up the long drive to Mrs Beasley's sprawling mansion. The sun was shining, the birds were singing, and all was right with the world. Maudie did feel a bit awkward about their meeting; Cora Beasley had been gracious enough at the time over Charlie's misdemeanor but today she had stressed 'just you, Nurse' when summoning Maudie to tea. Surely it was no coincidence that this was a Saturday, when Dick would normally be off-duty. Charlie could be left with Daddy.

'Do come in, Nurse! I'm so glad you were able to come. I want to discuss my latest plan with you before I go any further.'

Maudie's heart plummeted to her scuffed Clark's sandals; at least that was how it seemed for a moment. She had become embroiled in Cora Beasley's grand plans before. What was it this time? First aid classes for the Mothers' Union? Nutrition classes for unwed mothers? She had done her bit this past spring, instructing a dozen enthusiastic Girl Guides who wanted to earn a Child Care badge. The classes had been a success but Charlie had objected to having his napkin pinned and unpinned so many times and his roars had been deafening. Never again!

'I do believe it is time we started up those Mother and Baby afternoons again,' Mrs Beasley said when they were sipping China tea, which was no favourite of Maudie's. She preferred a good old black brew that would give a person a lift.

'I thought they were already doing that in the surgery.' Some years previously Mrs Beasley had converted the former gatehouse on her estate to a doctor's surgery and Maudie had even worked there herself during her time as a midwife.

'I'm sorry to say it fell through. We're a bit out of the way here and people have to hang about waiting for the bus, which doesn't always arrive on time, and you know yourself that isn't easy with a baby, especially if it's raining. But it was such a good idea, providing somewhere for young mothers to go, where they can have a cup of tea and chat to other women. Being at home with young children can be so isolating for a mother, particularly if it's her first child.'

Maudie knew all about it! 'And where exactly do I come in?'

'I've spoken to the vicar and he is in agreement that we move the event to the parish hall. What do you do on Wednesday afternoons, Nurse?'

'Er . . .'

'I thought as much. This couldn't be more convenient for you, could it? The hall is just up the road from your home, but you know that.' Of course Maudie knew that. Hadn't her little office been in the hall for all those years?

'What I'm trying to say is that many of the women are in the same boat. They live within walking distance of the parish hall and the sessions will end in time for them to go and meet their older children at the end of the school day. Those who come from the outlying districts will be able to call in at the shop before they catch the bus home, which will an added incentive to take part.'

'Wednesday is early closing at the shop.'

'Oh, is it? Perhaps Mrs Hatch can be persuaded to change her hours.'

Or perhaps not, Maudie thought, grinning to herself. She could just imagine the scene if those two determined women came together to fight that one out! Hammer and tongs wouldn't be in it! 'Perhaps the vicar can suggest a different day,' she murmured. 'As for me, I do agree that the idea is a good one, although I'm afraid I can't really see myself taking part.'

'Why ever not? It would suit you down to the ground.'

'The fact is, Mrs Beasley, I'm in my forties. I don't have a lot in common with women in their teens and twenties. And at the risk of sounding conceited, I don't need lectures in the right way to put on a nappy, or the advantages of making your own pureed fruit! I'm a trained nurse and a midwife, after all.'

'But of course you are, Nurse! Didn't I explain? I'm asking you to lead the group, not to participate as a learner. You might provide the odd demonstration, if it's called for, but mainly you'll be there as a resource person, someone the mothers can come to for advice, while their friends are drinking their tea. And surely you could lead the toddlers in some simple games while their mothers look on, or teach some songs or nursery rhymes to the little ones?'

Mrs Beasley beamed at Maudie, who had the unworthy thought that if the older woman thought all this was such a brilliant idea she should be running it herself! But she and Dick owed Cora Beasley a lot, for she had stepped in to enable them to buy their cottage at a price they could afford, at a time when the council had hoped to sell it to the highest bidder.

'I shall have to discuss it with Dick, of course, but I'll see what I can do. As you say, the parish hall is just round the corner and if little lord Charlie kicks up a fuss in the middle of it all I can always take him home before he brings the ceiling down.'

'I knew I could rely on you, Nurse!' Mrs Beasley smiled sweetly. 'And of course dear little Charlie won't cause a problem. How could you even think it?'

Maudie peered at her hostess, suspecting irony, but no, she appeared to be utterly sincere! How very odd. Cycling home again Maudie felt rejuvenated, thinking of all she might do to liven up the Wednesday sessions. She would thumb through Charlie's Mother Goose book and commit to memory any of the nursery rhymes she didn't know. 'Jack and Jill went up the hill, to fetch a pail of water' she chanted as she bounced along the lane, scaring a large tom cat who had been hunting for mice in the verges. He streaked across her path, making her brake suddenly, but she managed to keep her balance and continued on.

She was delighted at the prospect of something interesting to do. In many cases the women she'd be seeing knew her well, even if some of them were close to half her age. Other midwives might have brought their current babies into the world, yet she herself had delivered their older children, who would now be of school age. It would be lovely to hear of their progress.

Thinking of the infants' school made her draw her brows together in a frown. She thought about Verity Bourne and the luckless Eddie. She'd love to know how that unhappy relationship was progressing.

11

Maudie didn't have long to wait in order to find out. As she fumbled with the latch on the garden gate she heard voices drifting out through the open windows of the sitting room, which overlooked the village street. Feminine laughter, followed by Dick's deeper tones. What was that woman doing here? And how could she have known that the coast would be clear for her to pop in while Maudie was away?

Carefully fastening the gate behind her with Charlie in mind, Maudie wheeled her bike to the tool shed and put it away, thinking furiously. Should she appear nonchalantly as though she believed that Verity Bourne was no threat to her marriage? Or should she swoop down like an avenging angel, embarrassing all three of them? Play it cool, she told herself, quoting a character she'd seen in a Hollywood movie.

'I'm ho-ome!' she trilled, letting herself

in through the scullery door.

'In here,' Dick called. 'We've got company.'

Verity Bourne was sitting in Maudie's own special armchair, bold as brass. Dick sat opposite to her, looking guilty. Maudie bent down to kiss his cheek. She might as well publicly stake her claim.

'Charlie all right? Where is he, anyway?'

'Upstairs, sound asleep. He wore himself out, romping around with Rover.' Rover, too, seemed worn out. Even though there was no fire in the grate he was stretched out on the hearth rug, snoring gently, now and then giving a small hiccup.

Ungrateful beast! his mistress thought. *Why can't you come and bring your dinner up over that woman's fancy red shoes?* But Rover slept on.

'Of course the boy is all right,' Verity said, 'with his big brave policeman Daddy to take care of him.'

Oh, please! Maudie groaned inwardly. *Keep this up and you'll have me sicking up over your feet in a minute, never mind my dog. And why are you smirking like that, Dick Bryant?*

Dick seemed to sense that all was not well. 'How did you get on with Cora Beasley, love? She hasn't got you roped into one of schemes, has she?'

'Yes, she has, actually, but I think it's one I'll enjoy. She wants to revive the mother and baby afternoons, only in the village hall this time, not up at the gatehouse. I'll be the group leader, and Charlie will enjoy playing alongside the other toddlers, I'm sure.'

'What will that involve, being group leader?'

'Oh, you know, being there to deal with any concerns the other mothers may have, and getting the children involved in some simple games and community singing.'

'Really, Mrs Bryant!' Verity sneered. 'Are you sure that won't be too much for you?'

'I don't know what you mean, Miss Bourne.'

'Well, trying to teach children. That's an art, you know.'

'I didn't realize one had to go to teachers' college in order to belt out a few nursery rhymes, Miss Bourne. As it happens I've known *Mary Had Little Lamb* since I was knee-high to a grasshopper.'

Dick stood up hastily. 'Why don't I go and make a fresh brew and we'll have a some of that delicious cake Miss Bourne has kindly brought us?'

For the first time Maudie noticed a heavily iced chocolate cake sitting on the table. She noted with satisfaction that it seemed to be leaning to one side. That piece of work would never find favour at the Women's Institute Spring Fayre.

'What's the occasion?' she asked.

Miss Bourne simpered. 'I was so sorry for poor Dick having to miss the goodies on Coronation Day, so I thought I'd make it up to him.'

'A whole cake, just for Dick, when it isn't even his birthday!'

'That isn't till next month,' Dick put in.

Miss Bourne clasped her hands together. 'Next month! We must throw you a party. How old will you be, Dick?'

'Um, fifty,' he mumbled.

'The big Five-o! Then we must

definitely give you a party!' She turned to Maudie. 'Isn't it marvelous the way men only get better-looking as they age? Why, Dick is quite distinguished with his hair turning silver at the edges. It's not fair, really, when middle-aged women only get more and more dowdy and nobody ever gives them a second look.'

Right, Madam, that does it. The sight of her husband preening himself brought Maudie to her feet, but later she never knew what she might have done next because the doorbell rang, returning her to her senses.

A man stood on the doorstep, looking vaguely familiar. 'Mrs Bryant? Maudie? Have I come to the right place?'

'Jerry? Is it you? Just don't stand there, come on in!'

While Maudie introduced the two men, who somewhat hesitantly shook hands, Verity Bourne looked the newcomer up and down as if there was a bad smell under her nose. Maudie had to admit that poor Jerry hadn't worn well. The shirt cuffs that protruded from the sleeves of his wrinkled jacket could have done with mending, and when he turned to give a polite little bow to Verity it was obvious that the seat of his trousers was shiny with wear. His shoes needed mending, if not throwing out altogether.

But it was Jerry himself who looked tired and drab. His face was lined and his eyes looked haunted. His hair was well on the way to turning completely white. What on earth had happened to Jerry Saunders since she'd seen him last? He was even younger than Dick, yet what a difference there was between them. It was enough to break a person's heart.

'Aren't you going to introduce us, Mrs Bryant?' That was Verity, of course. Maudie felt suddenly protective of Jerry. If that awful woman dared to come out with one of her snide remarks, she would . . . well, she didn't know what she might do!

'I knew Mr Saunders when I was a girl,' she said. 'Our families were neighbours in those days.'

'An old flame, is he? Come to look you up? My goodness, Dick will have to look to his laurels now, won't he!'

'I'm sorry you can't stay, Miss Bourne,'

Maudie said firmly. 'I haven't seen Mr Saunders since long before the war, so naturally we have a lot of catching up to do. Thank you so much for baking us that cake. I'll see you out, shall I?'

Taking Verity by the elbow she propelled her towards the hall. Jerry looked from one of them to the other in puzzlement but, seeing that no explanation was offered, he turned to Dick and murmured something about the weather. Having shut the door behind Verity with a bang, Maudie re-entered the room, head held high.

'What happened to that cup of tea you were going to make, Dick? I'm sure Mr Saunders could do with one. And I'm not sure what to make of that cake your friend brought, but it was a kind thought on her part and we mustn't let it go to waste.' *And when Jerry has gone back to the Spread Eagle, she promised herself, what is left of that cake is going straight in the waste bin, and not one crumb of it will my son get to taste!*

* * *

The reunion with Jerry Saunders was not as awkward as Maudie had feared. She did manage to draw out of him the fact that his health wasn't good, mainly due to the time he had spent in a Japanese prisoner of war camp, although he refused to dwell on that now. Nor did he have much to say about his job, beyond the fact that it was a living, and he was glad to have found anything at all, considering the state he'd been in when released from hospital.

So much of the time was spent in the sort of 'do you remember when' talk that flows between old friends who haven't seen each other for decades. Dick listened politely, asking a question now and then, but he obviously wasn't interested, and by no stretch of the imagination could the reunion be called a success.

Maudie was thankful when loud cries were heard from upstairs, giving Jerry his cue to say that it had all been great but he must be going. Dick raised an eyebrow at her which she correctly interpreted as a question of were they going to invite Jerry to stay for tea, but she only agreed that it had indeed been lovely and they must do it again when he was next passing through Llandyfan. She had had enough for one day and she still had Charlie to see to.

'Shouldn't we have at least offered the chap a lift back to the pub?' Dick asked, when the door had closed behind Jerry Saunders. 'He looks like a feather could knock him over.'

'He'll be all right, Dick. He's tougher than he looks. Always was.' Yawning, she started towards the stairs.

12

The next day was fine so Maudie set out for the vicarage, to return a book to Joan Blunt. Both women were fans of Daphne Du Maurier's novels and Maudie had already exhausted the supply that was available at the Midvale library and was borrowing them for the second time. That being the case she was delighted when Mrs Blunt offered to lend her *The King's General*, which she hadn't come across before.

'This will tide me over nicely,' she said. 'I tried to get hold of *My Cousin Rachel* again but apparently there's a long waiting list for it.'

'It's always the way with recent releases, isn't it. I think you'll enjoy this one, although it's a little different from the others, being a blend of fact and fiction. I know it sounds greedy, Nurse, but if I'd married a rich man I'd have filled our house with books. I do love a good read!'

So Maudie had taken the book home and enjoyed it so much that she'd read it twice. She had even suggested to Dick that he might like to read it as well, but he'd shaken his head quite firmly, saying that he'd stick to Bulldog Drummond or the Saint, thanks very much. Now *The King's General* had to go back to its rightful owner, she told herself, and not before time.

Now, with Charlie in the pushchair and Rover running ahead, holding his tail aloft, she took her usual short cut through the graveyard. Pratt, the sexton, was busy doing something under the big yew tree, and nearby another man seemed to be browsing among the tombstones. Some of them were very old and the inscriptions made interesting reading.

The man saw her and waved. When she halted he came stumbling across the grass towards her, and she realized that it was Jerry Saunders.

'Hello, Jerry! I thought you'd have been far away by now.'

'No, I find myself with a couple of days between calls so I've stayed on. I must say they make you quite comfortable at the Spread Eagle.'

'So you've come to see our local church. It's very old, you know; mainly Norman. Also the village is believed to have been funded by a Celtic monk or saint who came here from Wales.'

'I wondered how it came by its name. It sounds more Welsh than English.'

'Dada!' The silence that followed this less than sparkling conversation was broken when Charlie decided that his mother had ignored him long enough. Perhaps in his mind he thought that Dada was a word applicable to any man, for certainly Jerry Saunders could never be mistaken for Dick.

'Is this your little boy?'

'Yes, that's right. This is Charles Richard Bryant, commonly known as Charlie. Look, if we're going to chat, shall we sit down? There's a bench over there.'

'I don't mind if I do. I'm feeling a bit groggy this morning and no, I haven't been drinking, Maudie. The fact is, I've never really recovered from the war; not one hundred per cent.'

'I'm sorry to hear that, Jerry. Were you wounded?'

'Not physically. Let's just say I saw sights that nobody should ever have to witness, not outside of a horror film. You know what the poet said about man's in-humanity to man; didn't we learn that at Oak Street council school? Well, I've seen it all, Maudie, seen it all. I've looked into the pit and seen the devil laughing back, trying to catch me with his pitchfork.'

Maudie didn't quite know what to say in answer to this. It seemed a bit extreme, somehow. She waited.

'I think I mentioned that I spent a long time as a prisoner of war in a Japanese prison camp, and it was only because of you that I came through it alive,' he said at last.

'Me? What did I do?' She'd written to a few boys, just so they'd have cheery letters from home while they were in the services, but she didn't recall Jerry having been one of them.

'When we were made to watch our friends being tortured and killed I used to close my eyes and see you instead,

Maudie. That was all that kept me sane, knowing you were here to come back to.'

'Oh Jerry!'

'Oh, don't worry. I know you weren't waiting for me. I knew there was no future for us as a couple, but just knowing you were somewhere in England, sweet and clean and free, was all I needed. That's what we'd been fighting for, you see, and that's why I find comfort in looking at old stones in a country churchyard like this one. No doubt the people buried here had their troubles, but they lived and died in a saner world.'

Maudie was touched. 'So what happened to you after the war was over, Jerry?'

'After we came back to England I went looking for our old house, but the whole terrace was gone. Bombed to smithereens. It gave me a bad shock, seeing that. I finally found Mum. She'd gone to live with her sister in Worthing before it happened.'

'How did you manage to trace me, then, Jerry?'

He smiled suddenly, and for a brief

moment Maudie caught a glimpse of the boy she used to know.

'That was a bit of luck, really. When I came to stay at the pub here, lo and behold there was a picture of you on the wall in the bar!'

Maudie remembered that. It was a newspaper clipping that Len Frost had framed, a photo taken by the Midvale *Chronicle* after she had helped to catch a criminal.

'I want to ask you something,' Jerry said suddenly.

'Yes?'

'That woman I met yesterday at your home. You don't care for her, do you?'

Might as well be honest, she thought. She wrinkled her nose and growled in her throat, making Charlie laugh.

'Has she done something to hurt you, Maudie? Only I could see that you wanted to get rid of her and that's not like you. Leastways, it's not like the girl I used know, who wouldn't be unkind to a soul.'

Maudie laughed sheepishly. 'It's something and nothing. I really shouldn't rise to it but I can't seem to help myself. Verity Bourne is one of those women who like to sidle up to every man she meets, laying the flattery on with a knife. That wouldn't be so bad in itself — most men can look after themselves and I suppose they enjoy a mild flirtation — but it's the way she treats other women. She's already implied, even stated outright, that I'm dowdy, uninteresting, incapable of teaching nursery rhymes to children and a hopeless mother. And of course she's so sorry for poor Dick, being married to an idiot like me.'

'I didn't see any sign of your husband falling for it; at least, not while I was there, which admittedly was for a very short time. Is he likely to let you down?'

'Oh, I don't think so. He may be flattered by her attention, though. I'm really not sure about that.'

'Then why were you so tense?'

Maudie felt that this conversation had gone far enough. 'Because the dratted woman baked my husband a cake, and called round with it when I was away from home. Now it's been lovely talking to you, Jerry, but I really must be going. I'm on my way to the vicarage and if I don't get there soon my friend won't have time to talk to me before she has to start getting her husband's lunch.'

'And I must make my way back to the Spread Eagle and do my packing. I'm moving on in the morning, Maudie.' He hesitated for a long moment, and then reached out and grasped her hand. She moved away a little, afraid he would try to kiss her. 'I can't tell you what it has meant to me, seeing you again. I've always wondered where you ended up and it seemed like a miracle when I saw that photograph of you, a miracle. I must have been guided here, that's all I can say.'

Maudie continued on her way, feeling like a heel to have cut him off so abruptly. But the encounter had been far too emotional, and in its own way hadn't it been something similar to Verity's pursuit of Dick? It was quite apparent that Jerry's wartime experiences had affected him deeply. The Jerry Saunders she had known in her youth had not been such a bag of nerves. She might have described him as plodding, reliable, stolid, faithful: any one of those things, but now he was fundamentally changed.

Should she be doing anything to try to help him? Or would such interference cause trouble all round? Should she mention any of this to Dick, or would it be wise to keep her thoughts to herself? She strode on, deeply troubled.

13

Maudie entered the village shop, pleased to find that she was the only customer. Ever since that horrible day when Charlie had been snatched from his pram she never left him outside while she shopped, although carrying him on her hip was a nuisance. She dared not put him down on the floor because he would make short work of the items on the lower shelves. At home his greatest joy was to rootle through the kitchen cupboards where Maudie stored her saucepans so he could hardly be blamed for attacking brightly coloured objects here.

'My goodness, he's getting to be a big boy, isn't he?' Mrs Hatch said, beaming. 'Two years old now. How time flies! And I never gave him anything for his birthday! Would he like a bar of c-h-o-c, Nurse?'

No, thank you,' Maudie said hastily. 'It's very kind of you, but he loves c-h-o-c and if he gets to know where it comes from he'll be after you for more every time we come to the shop. I'd rather keep it as a very occasional treat.'

'And I suppose he can't have a bit of barley sugar in case he chokes on it,' Mrs Hatch said. 'Never mind, I expect it will be his dinner time soon, and we don't want to spoil his appetite. What can I do for you today, then, Nurse?'

'I just wanted to hand in my order,' Maudie told her, fumbling in her pocket for her list. 'Dick will call in for it at the weekend, unless you've got a new delivery boy?'

'No such luck. Delivery boys are a vanishing breed, it seems. Since the war they've all got ideas above their station, that's what.'

Maudie's thoughts flew back to her own youth, when Jerry Saunders had started out in the working world riding an old black sit-up-and-beg bike. As if on cue, Mrs Hatch simpered and said, 'You've had a visit from an old flame, I hear.'

'Hardly that, Mrs Hatch. Just someone I went to school with. Our grandmothers were close friends, so we were in and out of each other's houses a great deal.'

Could someone you'd merely walked around the town with be called an old flame? They might have been to the pictures together once or twice, sitting in the cheapest seats, but it hardly made for a great romance, did it?

'I'll believe you, Nurse! Thousands wouldn't!'

'I'm afraid that Mr Saunders had a rough war, Mrs Hatch. He was a prisoner of war in a Japanese camp, and it looks to me as if his health has been undermined by the experience. His not the cheerful boy I used to know.'

'Ah, I've heard such stories, Nurse! It was criminal the way them boys of ours was treated. Still, it will do the man good to talk about old times. Is he coming back to see you again? Does your hubby mind?'

Maudie didn't want to go down that road! Mrs Hatch was a goodhearted soul, but people said that her tongue was hinged in the middle and loose at both ends. If you knew what was good for you it was wise not to give her any fuel for gossip.

'By the way, I had a word with Miss Bourne,' she said.

'Then I hope you gave her what for! Slashing a poor little lad's hands like that! I do wish she'd go back where she came from, and no mistake!'

'I do agree that her treatment was far too harsh for a child of that age, but I'm afraid that he did merit some sort of punishment. According to her the boy is quite unmanageable and if he's going to profit from her teaching at all he has to be brought into line.'

'Then put him in the corner, not lash out at him. I spent hours sitting in the corner with a dunce cap on, and it didn't do me no harm.'

'I don't know about a dunce cap, but she has tried sitting him in the corner, to no effect. Apparently he's been biting the smaller children and that can't go on.'

'Well, I must say I never thought you'd side with that Miss Bourne, Nurse. I'm surprised, I am really!'

'Oh, I'm not on her side at all, Mrs

Hatch. Far from it. Now, I'd better be going. I'm due at the mother and baby group in half and hour, and by the feel of things I'll have to call in at home and find Charlie a dry pair of trousers.'

★   ★   ★

The first meeting of the MAB, as the women dubbed it, was a great success. Maudie could see the mothers visibly relaxing as they sipped their tea and exchanged tales with each other. So many of them were isolated in their farm homes with their young children that they seldom had the chance to remember that they were women first. Perhaps it would be possible to bring someone in to demonstrate make-up techniques to the group, while one or two of their number kept the children amused.

Young Mrs Pritchard was a natural when it came to leading the kiddies in action songs. Even Charlie sat on the floor paying attention by waving his little arms in time to the music. This gave Maudie the opportunity to circulate, exchanging a few words with each mother.

Some of them also had children of five or six, who were pupils at the village school. She was alarmed to hear more complaints about Miss Bourne, and she listened carefully to what was being said. She really mustn't let her personal feelings of animosity towards the woman colour her viewpoint, but if the infants' teacher really was a danger to the children something must be done about it. Both Cora Beasley and the vicar were on the school's board of governors and she could always have a quiet word with one of them.

'She wouldn't let my Freddie go out to the lavs,' one woman said. 'He told me he put his hand up, nice as pie, but she said he should have gone before he came into class, and now he had to wait until playtime. The poor little scrap had to sit there in agony until he wet himself. I ask you, is that any way to treat a beginner at the school? All the other kiddies jeered at him, said he was a baby. Now he's taken against the school and I have an awful job getting him out of bed in the morning.'

'Same here!' another mother chimed

in. 'I kept my Jeanie at home for a couple of days when she had a streaming cold. Well, I know you're supposed to send an excuse note on the first day back, but I didn't have no time to write one, what with all I have to do of a morning, getting my hubby off to work and that. Well, that woman, that Miss Bourne, she kept our Jeanie in for half an hour after school, saying it would teach her to bring a note the next time. When I went up the school to meet the children I was a few minutes late, and when our Jeanie wasn't there I almost had a heart attack, thinking something must have happened to her. I come over all queer, I did.'

The woman turned to Maudie. 'You'll know how I felt, won't you, Nurse? I heard about your boy being snatched last year. It's a mother's worst nightmare. She shouldn't be allowed to keep a child in without telling the parents what's going on. Especially not a kiddie like my Jeanie, who's too young to understand.'

A rumble of agreement went through the little group. The assembled women looked at Maudie expectantly. She groaned inwardly. If she were elected to go and tackle the teacher a second time, Verity would no doubt assume that she was getting under Maudie's skin because of the attention she was paying to Dick. And in this game of female one upmanship there was no way that she must be allowed to win. It did appear that Miss Bourne was unfit to be in charge of very young children, but what if Maudie were instrumental in getting Miss Bourne the sack? She had a nasty idea that Dick was flattered by the awful woman's flirtatious advances and although he was unlikely to succumb to her charms he might think less of his wife for going go such lengths to put a spoke in her wheel.

'Go on, Nurse, you can do it!' A little cheer went up and Maudie caved in.

'All right. I'll go and have a word with the vicar, and see what he can do.'

'That's right, Nurse! Another few years and your Charlie will be going to that school. You wouldn't want her for his teacher, would you?'

Maudie shook her head vigourously. She certainly wouldn't want that!

14

The vicar looked at Maudie with a look of reproach in his tired grey eyes. 'I don't think I quite understand you, Nurse Bryant. We must have discipline in our schools. It is there that the seeds of future success will be sown. You are a trained nurse; suppose you and your fellow trainees had entered the hospital having no regard for the respect due to your superiors there; for the carrying out of the proper methods of treatment for your patients? How long would you have lasted? And surely those superiors would have expected you to come to them amenable to discipline, having learned proper behaviour by the example set by your parents and teachers?'

'Quite so, Mr Blunt, and of course the older children must be taught right from wrong. But we are speaking of very young children, many of them away from home for the first time and just getting their first taste of the wider world. Little ones of five and six years old. That's why it's known as an infants' school, after all.'

'Give me a child until he is seven and I will give you the man,' the vicar said.

Maudie was amazed to hear a Church of England priest quoting Jesuit philosophy, but she pressed on nevertheless.

'I think you should know that we may soon have a rebellion on our hands,' she told him. 'The mothers are up in arms, and the last I heard a few of them are planning to make signs and march up to the school in protest. You can imagine the scandal should the *Midvale Chronicle* get hold of this! Their reporters and photographers would have a field day. Can you imagine the headlines? Teacher thrashes infant pupil. 'My baby came home in tears, says mother'. Angry parents picket Llandyfan School.'

'Very well, Nurse. Don't get carried away. It is very much against my principles, but I shall have a word with Miss Bourne and see if she can't be persuaded to modify her approach a little.' He strode out of the room, looking aggrieved.

What's eating him? Maudie thought. *It's not like him to be so rude.* She hoped he wasn't losing his faith or something. That would indeed be a disaster.

* * *

'Oh, don't mind him,' Joan Blunt said, passing Maudie a cup of coffee. 'He's just got a bad case of the Miss Bournes, that's all.'

'What on earth do you mean?'

'Only that she's been doing her best to wrap him round her little finger with her flirty ways and middle-aged men are unfortunately susceptible to things like that. He catches himself smiling back and thinking himself no end of a fellow, and then he comes to his senses and feels ashamed.'

'Oh.'

'Not your Dick as well?'

'Yes, unfortunately. She's not even very subtle about it. She even brought him a homemade cake the other day, if you can believe that!'

'Was it any good?'

119

'I didn't taste it. I binned it as soon as she'd gone. I wouldn't even let Rover have it.'

'Chocolate isn't good for dogs,' Mrs Blunt retorted and for some reason the pair of them found that very finny and they laughed and gulped until the tears ran down their faces.

* * *

Dick burst into the house, looking furious. Maudie looked at him in surprise.

'What's the matter with you, Dick Bryant: bad day at work?'

'You could say that! I got a proper rocket from the chief!'

'That doesn't sound like him.' DI Bob Goodman was the mildest of men, always willing to hear both sides of a story before pronouncing judgment.

'You know his views about us getting personal calls at work, unless it's an emergency.'

'Well, yes, but I didn't phone the station today. Did someone say that I did?'

'That dratted woman had the nerve to

call up and tell the WPC on switchboard that she wanted to make arrangements for a fiftieth birthday party for me!'

'Good grief!'

'She insisted on being put through to the chief, babbling some nonsense about where the party should be held. Is the station big enough, or should she hire a hall? And the worse of it is that Bob was already in a bad mood being in the middle of compiling the quarterly crime statistics.'

'I don't believe this!'

'Neither did the chief. I tried to explain that this is just some stupid idea she's got into her head, nothing to do with me at all, but that didn't wash with our respected leader! He said what was the use of my being on the force and trying to bring criminals to justice if I couldn't keep just one lovesick woman under control? I tell you, Maudie; I didn't know where to look!'

'Someone should strangle that woman!' Maudie muttered, not for the first time.

'And now the rest of the lads are taking the mickey, right, left and centre! 'Here comes lover boy, ha ha. He may be fifty but he's not over the hill yet.' I could strangle the idiot woman myself.'

Out of the corner of her eye Maudie thought she saw something moving outside the open window. She hoped they weren't about to get another visit from Verity Bourne. That would be all they needed. She went to the window and looked out, but the street was empty. Probably someone racing past on a bicycle, she thought.

'Never mind, I'm sure this will all blow over,' she told Dick. 'Tea will be ready soon. Why don't you nip up and have your wash while you wait? And you might look in on Charlie while you're at it. If he's wide awake you may as well bring him down with you when you come. I'll let him have a rusk to keep him happy while we have our own meal.'

'Right-ho, but I have something to tell you first. The fact is, I'm being sent to Scotland.'

'Scotland?' she squeaked. 'Tell me you're not being transferred!' It was true that she had always longed to see that country with its glorious scenery and fascinating history, but as a visitor, not a permanent resident. Llandyfan was home to her now, and besides they owned this cottage. The thought of selling up and moving away was too much to bear.

'Calm down, old girl! I'm only being sent to a conference to learn how their coppers do things there. Did you know that Scottish law is quite different from English law?' Before they were married Dick had received similar training in Canada, all part of seeing how law enforcement was carried out in other countries and perhaps adopting some of those methods as a result.

'Where is this conference being held?'

'Edinburgh.'

'Oh, Dick! I have to see it. I've read so much about it! Can I come with you?'

'Sorry, love; no wives. But I tell you what we'll do. Perhaps we could manage a holiday up there some summer when Charlie is a little older. Hire a little caravan and go touring. Rover could come with us then.'

Maudie tried to swallow her disappointment. She had been mad to think she could go to Edinburgh now, with a dog and a two-year-old in tow. The country might have gone through two devastating wars but nothing much had changed for women, had it? Men went out and experienced the cut and thrust of life in the world outside, while their wives remained at home, awaiting their return.

She brightened. Dick's absence would at least solve the Verity Bourne problem, albeit temporarily. The woman could hardly follow him to Edinburgh, could she? She might, of course, arrange to have a brass band playing at the station to welcome him home when he stepped off the train. That was pure fantasy, of course, but Maudie would take jolly good care that no word of what was being planned for Dick should come to the school teacher's ears.

'Do go up,' she told her husband. 'My nose tells me that the baked potatoes are just about done, and as soon as I heat up some corned beef I'll be ready to dish up.' Dick was partial to corned beef which suited Maudie very well, because it was so easy to prepare. Just open the can with the little key that came with it and use the meat in one of any number of different ways. 'And apple dumplings to follow!'

'With lemon sauce?'

'And stuffed with raisins.'

'Good-oh! Shan't be a tick!' He took the stairs two at a time.

A glad cry of 'Dada' greeted his arrival, followed by a long string of unintelligible words. Smiling, Maudie went to attend to her duties in the kitchen. As the poet had put it so well, God was in His heaven and all was right with her world. Well, almost.

15

Maudie stared sadly at her beloved red dress. She had brought it out again, still hoping that she could let it out a bit but it was clearly impossible. The bodice buttoned all the way down to the waist and that gave her an idea. What if she sewed it shut on the inside? It couldn't gape open then. Would she be able to get it on over her head in that case? She would have to tack it firmly together first, to make sure.

The doorbell rang. Cursing, she put the frock on the table and went to answer the door. Verity Bourne rushed past her, red-faced and furious.

'Was it you who shopped me to the vicar?' she demanded.

Maudie stuck out her chin. 'I did speak to Mr Blunt, yes, but only because some of the mothers asked me to do so. They are deeply concerned . . . '

'Deeply concerned my aunt fanny! All they care about is getting those kids off their hands so they can laze about all day, drinking tea and gossiping. I'm the one who has to deal with their undisciplined children and then they dare to criticize me when I have to step in where they've failed.'

'That's not fair, Miss Bourne.' Maudie shut the front door with a bang. 'I know these women. Most of them work very hard, with little money to go on. And they are genuinely fond their children and try to do their best for them. And you must realize that with the best will in the world, it takes time for children to get used to the very different world of school. They need patience and understanding at first.'

'What would you know about it?' Verity sneered. 'You've never had a child in school, have you? That disobedient little boy of yours has got a shock coming when he starts school. I shall have my work cut out getting him licked into shape when he does.'

'Over my dead body!' Maudie bawled. Glancing out of the open window she saw that two women clutching shopping baskets had stopped to listen. She really mustn't shout like a fishwife when people might be passing by. She lowered her voice. 'Why have you come, Miss Bourne? If you've quite finished I must ask you to leave. I have a very busy day ahead of me.'

'I told you. I wanted to find out if it was you who went tattling to Mr Blunt. He called on me at my lodgings and gave me a reprimand that was quite uncalled for.'

'He didn't give you your marching orders, then?'

'No, he did not. And I'm warning you, Mrs Bryant! Any more interference from you and there will be serious repercussions.' She stalked to the door, jerking it open so that the letterbox rattled and ran off, almost knocking over a newcomer in the process.

'I say, I hope I haven't come at a bad time,' Jerry Saunders said.

'Not at all. Do come in. Right now I could use a friend.

'I thought you'd left,' she began, when they were sitting at the table.

'So I had, but when I got to Dillchester I found that the shop I was supposed to visit had closed. They've gone bust and nobody thought to let us know.'

'I'm sorry.'

'Oh well, it gives me a couple of extra days' holiday before my next port of call, so I thought I might as well come back to your local. Your husband won't object to my calling round again, I hope?'

'I shouldn't think so, but in any case he's away right now.'

'On police business, I expect.'

'That's right. Tell me more about yourself, Jerry. What made you decide to become a travelling salesman?'

He shrugged. 'I had to make a living somehow, and nobody else would have me. You may know that when I joined up old Fred at the grocer's promised me my job back after the war, but that didn't pan out. When I came home I found that Fred had died and the shop had been sold. It's a second hand bookshop now.'

'I'm sorry,' she said again.

'I didn't mind, not really. I'm a bit long in the tooth to be delivering groceries on a bike.'

'Surely they'd have had a van by now.

That's if it had still been a grocer's shop.'

'And I drive a company car today, so it's all the same to me.'

'You learned to drive in the army, did you?'

'I did, but I don't like to talk about those days, Maudie. Tell me about that woman who was here just now. She's come bothering you again, hasn't she?'

'I suppose I had it coming,' she told him. 'As I said last time she's been coming down hard on the little ones she's in charge of at the school and the mothers asked me to speak to the vicar about it. He's on the board of governors, you see. I had a reputation for being a Miss Fixit when I was the district midwife here. Mr Blunt wasn't keen to get involved but apparently he did go and say something and now of course she blames me.'

Their talk drifted into a trip down memory lane then, as they recalled their own far-off schooldays with teachers who were now either retired or gone to their reward.

'They were good days, weren't they, Maudie? We didn't have much in the way of worldly goods but we made our own pleasures.'

'Were they such good days, Jerry? Your father, getting killed in the war, and mine coming back with his leg off. Our mums working every hour of the day to put food on the table, and having to make every sixpence do the work of a shilling.'

'Compared with what I've seen since it seems like paradise. You and me, taking those long walks in the rain, then coming home to your place and feasting on toast and dripping. Life doesn't get any better than that.'

This was dangerous talk. Maudie was prepared to welcome Jerry into her home and to entertain him for an hour or two for old times' sake, but she didn't want him to moon over her as if something could come of it. The poor chap was obviously lonely but she wasn't going to let herself feel guilty. Just because they'd had a boy-girl relationship at a very young age that didn't mean she'd let him down in any way, all those years ago.

She attempted to steer their conversation into safer waters, but it wasn't easy.

131

What did he do in his spare time? Did he have any hobbies? Did he enjoy reading? Which football team did he support? Each query was followed by a sad shake of the head. Jerry Saunders appeared to have no interest in life whatsoever.

It was a relief when a series of wails came from upstairs, and Rover came to nudge Maudie's hand to alert her to her duties.

'That's my little boy, wanting to get up from his nap and wanting his lunch,' she said. 'I'm afraid I'll have to go and see to him.'

'That's quite all right. I'll go now. I mustn't outstay my welcome. Just remember one thing, Maudie. If that woman continues to worry you, you must stand firm. I don't like to think of you in distress.'

Maudie laughed. 'You don't need to worry about me! I'm more than capable of dealing with the like of her. Off you go, then, Jerry. Safe journey!' She escorted him to the door.

'That put paid to my morning,' she told Rover, who wagged his tail furiously in response. 'I know I shan't be able to settle to anything now after all that excitement, so we'll all go out for a nice long w-a-l-k this afternoon.' With Dick away, and no evening meal to prepare, she and Charlie could make do with scrambled eggs, which would be a treat.

Before going upstairs she retrieved her spotted dress from the table where she'd left it before going to answer the door. If Charlie found it and clutched it in his sticky fingers that would be the last straw. She would bring it out again some evening after he was in bed and work on it then, unless of course by any chance she'd managed to lose a few pounds in the meantime. Maudie liked to think she was optimistic by nature and it is a true saying that hope springs eternal in the human breast.

Howls of fury rent the air. 'All right, Charlie, hang on. Mummy's coming!' She sprinted up the stairs, pausing at the top to catch her breath.

At the door of the nursery she paused, wrinkling her nose. Charlie greeted her rapturously. He had managed to wriggle out of his nappy and had used the contents to decorate his cot and the nearby wall. He gave her an angelic smile.

She groaned, wondering what had happened to potty training. 'It's bath time for you, my lad! Up you come!' Just another day at Chez Bryant.

16

Maudie passed a blissful few days playing with Charlie and reading her library books. Let the house look after itself for a while; she was on holiday. Happily, life seemed to have returned to normal. She had heard nothing more from Verity Bourne, and she'd heard from Dora Frost that Jerry had left for points unknown. She hadn't even been over to have coffee with her friend, Joan Blunt, or for that matter expected her to come to the cottage, for she hoped to avoid the vicar for a while.

Midway through the week Dick phoned.

'What have you been up to?'

'Nothing much. Hiking round the countryside with Charlie and Rover. Reading books and eating chocolate. What have you been doing?'

'This and that. The conference sessions are quite interesting and the other chaps are all very friendly, but I'll be glad to get home. Sitting around in stuffy rooms makes me want to go to sleep.'

'Can't you cut it short, then, and hop on a train?'

'Afraid not,' Dick sighed. 'The chief wouldn't take it kindly if I opted out. Besides, I'm supposed to write up a report about the whole thing and I need to be here to get the details. I miss you, though. When I get back, what say we find someone to mind the son and heir, put our glad rags on and go out for a meal. Would you like that?'

'Lovely!'

'Listen, there go the pips and I don't have any more change so I'll have to go. See you soon. Love you.'

'Love you too.' The line went dead.

★ ★ ★

The banging on the front door was so urgent that Maudie guessed it must be some man trying to find a midwife for his labouring wife. If it was he was out of luck. She couldn't go bringing babies into the world with Charlie at her side.

She flung the door open to reveal a short, youngish woman whom she recognized from the Mother and Baby group.

'Oh, Nurse, you'll never guess what's happened!'

'No, what is it?'

'I was in the shop when we heard the news. Mrs Hatch sent me to fetch you. She said you'd want to know.'

'Calm down, Mrs Leeson, and try to talk slowly. What do I want to know?'

'It's that Miss Bourne, Nurse. A man walking his dog just found her, up the Glebe.'

Maudie swung into action. 'Wait here while I fetch my bag. I'm afraid you'll have to stay with my little boy, but I'll be back as soon as I can. Has Mrs Hatch called for an ambulance?'

'None of that won't do you no good, Nurse. She's a goner.'

'Dead? How do they know? Has a doctor seen her?'

'Bart Fellowes, the chap who found her, says it don't need no doctor to tell him she's dead. Strangled, she was, and her face all purple and her tongue . . . '

'Thank you, Mrs Leeson, I get the picture. You go back to the shop and I'll be along as soon as I can.'

* * *

Buttoning Charlie into a clean romper suit Maudie asked herself what she was doing, getting involved in this. Of course she was all agog to know what had happened; who wouldn't be? But she'd always despised what Dick referred to as 'ambulance chasers' and here she was, rushing to join in the speculation. True, she had heartily disliked the annoying teacher, yet she certainly wouldn't wish her dead. She should stay out of the investigation, as Dick would most certainly tell her to. On the other hand, she had been summoned by Mrs Hatch and it was her duty to go to the shop in case her help was needed to calm hysterical bystanders.

* * *

The shop was full of excited women when Maudie arrived. 'Thank goodness you've come, Nurse. Poor Ethel back there, when she heard what happened to poor Miss Bourne, she clutched at her heart and keeled right over, and we don't know what to do for her next.'

'Hold my child for me, if you wouldn't mind,' Maudie said, thrusting Charlie into the arms of one of the gaping onlookers. 'And for goodness' sake don't let him down on the floor, or he'll have everything off those shelves before you can blink an eye. Pass me the smelling salts, Mrs Hatch, and the rest of you stand back, please, and give the patient some air.'

Order was soon restored and the recumbent woman was transferred to the chair beside the counter and a cup of tea put into her hand. 'Now then,' said Maudie, 'what's all this I hear about Miss Bourne?'

'Bart Fellowes was the one who found her,' Mrs Hatch began. 'Up the glebe when he was walking that Missy. Or you might well say that Missy was walking him, for he's slower than a snail this days, and him a long-distance runner in years gone by. He tried to phone for help from the vicarage, but there was nobody home, and all the doors was shut tight. So he came here instead, and I dialled 999.'

'And he definitely found her dead, you say.'

'Oh, yes, Nurse. Strangled, she was, and her face all purple, and her tongue . . . '

'Yes, thank you. I know that bit.'

★   ★   ★

After a time an ambulance went by, moving slowly and without the bell ringing. That, more than anything else, was confirmation for the waiting crowd that the victim was dead.

'That's it then,' said Mrs Hatch. 'We shan't know any more until the police come calling. Your man is missing all the fun, Nurse, being away up in Scotland.'

'I'll hardly call it fun, Mrs Hatch. Miss Bourne wasn't popular, but she was a human being, and now she's dead. And whoever did it may not be far away. Don't you realize that we now have a killer in our midst? Somebody who may strike again at any moment?' A shudder went through the group and there was a general stampede for the door.

★ ★ ★

The police will have their work cut out for them this time, Maudie told herself, when she had reached home and locked herself and Charlie inside. Having looked under the bed for possible intruders who might be lying in wait, and checking the phone to make sure it was working properly, she sat down to think.

Because of her teaching philosophy, Verity Bourne hadn't been liked. But which of her detractors could have killed her? Certainly not the little band of mothers who had risen up against her, no matter what the provocation had been. Strangling was not a woman's crime, and in any case Verity was a tall woman and she wouldn't have been easy to strangle.

The killer was probably someone from her past, who had followed her to Llandyfan; a jilted lover, perhaps, or the

141

parent of a child who had died as a result of the teacher's negligence. This, of course, was the explanation everyone would prefer. An outsider. Someone who didn't belong. Anything other than it being one of their own.

The question that occurred to Maudie was what had Miss Bourne been doing at the glebe in the middle of the school day? The glebe was a large piece of land that belonged to the church. Stalls were set up there during the village fete, and school sports days were always held there, but for most of the year it lay fallow. People tended to use it as a short cut between the village proper and the recently built prefab cluster, but otherwise it was only frequented by dog walkers, courting couples and wandering children.

From time to time the vicar threatened to enclose it, citing possible court cases that could arise if someone had an accident on church land, but lack of money was the usual barrier to that and nothing was ever done.

★   ★   ★

The doorbell rang, startling Maudie out of a deep sleep. She sat up, looking around her in momentary confusion. Everything seemed to be in order. Charlie was safe inside his playpen, pushing some small cars to and fro. Rover, replete from his evening meal, simply raised his head for a moment before settling down again. The appetizing aroma of mulligatawny soup still lingered in the air.

The doorbell pealed again. Fumbling for her slippers and not finding them Maudie rolled off the settee and staggered to the door. Remembering what had happened earlier in the day she squinted through the spy hole to see if it was safe to open the door. Three people waited on the doorstep. Her heart skipped a beat when she recognized the taller of the two men, while the fact that they were accompanied by a WPC was even more ominous. She flung the door open.

'Is it Dick? Have you come to tell me that something's happened to Dick?'

'Your husband is quite all right, Mrs Bryant,' DCI Goodman said, strangely formal. 'May we come in?'

143

'Yes, of course. You'll have to excuse me. I was sound asleep until the doorbell woke me up.'

Introductions were made. The visitors sat down. Offers of tea or coffee were made, and refused. Maudie found her slippers and slid her feet into them.

'Mrs Bryant, I assume you've heard that the local infants' school teacher was found dead this morning.' DCI Goodman appeared stern, not at all like the genial chap she'd met on numerous social occasions.

'Verity Bourne. Yes. Someone came to fetch me because a customer at the village shop had passed out when she heard the news.'

'A relative of the dead woman?'

'Oh, I don't think so. Verity wasn't a local person. My understanding was that she came here from somewhere up north.'

'And I understand that the two of you — yourself and the victim — were not on the best of terms.'

'Well we were on opposite sides of a dispute, having to do with her treatment of pupils at the school. Some of the mothers asked me to approach the vicar, to make a complaint to him in his role as school governor, and that is what I did. Naturally Miss Bourne wasn't best pleased, and came here to tear me off a strip about it.'

'But that wasn't the only problem between you, Mrs Bryant. Isn't it true that she was trying to steal your husband from you? I spoke to her, you know, when she was attempting to organize a birthday gathering for Bryant. Quite a song and dance she gave me, about there being trouble between you and your husband and how she felt called to bolster the poor chap up.'

'Well, I say! How dare she? Dick and I are perfectly happy together. You can ask him yourself and see what he says.'

'That will come later. But you admit that Miss Bourne was trying to come between you, and naturally you resented it.'

'Of course I did, but that doesn't mean I killed her!'

The questions continued, with the policewoman sitting meekly by while the junior man jotted things down in his notebook.

'One last thing, Mrs Bryant. Do you perhaps own a red frock, or perhaps a skirt, with an overall pattern of white spots?'

Maudie's jaw dropped. 'You know I do. I was wearing it at your daughter's engagement party.'

'I'm afraid I don't notice things like that. My wife is always giving me a hard time about it. When I have to attend some official function she always wants to know what the ladies were wearing, and I'm unable to tell her. She calls me a right idiot.' The policewoman smirked.

'The thing is, Mrs Bryant — Maudie — the victim was strangled with a sort of belt, or sash, which is red with white spots. Does your frock have such an accessory?'

'Yes, it does. I can show you if you like. It's just upstairs.'

'Please, if you don't mind.'

Maudie flew upstairs and removed her dress from the cupboard. She fumbled for the tie belt but it wasn't there. The two empty loops at the waist, where it usually hung, were mute testimony to its absence. She hunted everywhere, just in case it had fallen off when she'd brought the garment upstairs, but it was nowhere to be found.

Sick at heart she returned to the living room, where she handed the dress to Bob Goodman. 'This is the dress, but I can't find the belt. It was here yesterday, lying right on that table. I can't think where it's got to.'

'I'm afraid we'll have to take this with us. Write out a receipt for Mrs Bryant, will you, Rawlings? This will be all for now, but I shall have to return later to question you further with your husband present. Do you understand, Mrs Bryant?'

Maudie nodded wordlessly, rooted to the floor like a statue. At least he hadn't warned her not to leave town and he hadn't enquired as to whether she possessed a passport.

After they had gone she sank into a chair, hardly able to believe what had just happened. The detestable Verity Bourne was dead, and Maudie was a suspect.

She wanted Dick. He would come and

get this sorted out! He had given her the number of the hotel where he was staying, but when she telephoned, the receptionist there was unable to help, having rung Dick's room and got no answer. 'I'm sorry, Madam, but their meetings are over for the day. No, none of them are in the bar; it's closed for redecoration. I expect they've gone out to a nice pub somewhere and they'll be back soon. If you'd care to try again later . . . '

'This is urgent,' said poor Maudie. 'Could you give me the numbers of the pubs in the district? I'll call them myself.'

The receptionist hesitated. 'Have you any idea how many pubs there are in Edinburgh, Madam?'

'No. I don't suppose I have. Thank you for your time.' Maudie flung herself across the bed as the tears came, thick and fast. Pulling the eiderdown across her shaking body she curled into a ball and prayed for sleep. Then she remembered Charlie, who was still in his playpen downstairs. She hauled herself off the bed and went to attend to her son.

17

Maudie spent the next day in seclusion. Leaving the phone off the hook gave her some peace, although the doorbell rang several times, making her jump. Peeping out from behind the drawn curtains she was able to see who her callers were and she was distressed to see that a reporter from the Midvale *Chronicle* had tried his luck more than once. She would have had to answer the door if DI Goodman had come back, but so far there was no word from him. She hoped he was following up new clues which didn't involve her. She desperately wished that Joan Blunt would come to offer sympathy; she needed her friend's reassurance but so far she had heard nothing.

She was badly shaken by the realization that the murder weapon — if you could call it that — might be her own belt. How could that be? And how on earth could she prove that she hadn't brought harm to Verity Bourne? Maudie had enough faith in the British justice system to believe that, if the case came to trial and she found herself in the dock, she would not be found guilty. They wouldn't hang an innocent person, would they? She pushed the thought out of her mind.

It was more likely that her reputation would be sullied. 'No smoke without fire' people would say. Some would be delighted to point a finger at her wherever she went, despite any evidence to the contrary. 'There goes that woman who strangled that poor little school teacher. She got off, of course, but what a scandal that was. It only goes to show what a clever barrister can do.'

Even worse would be the knowledge that she had unwittingly brought shame and ruin to her family. Dick's career would come to an abrupt halt; even if they kept him on the force he would never get promotion with a murder suspect for a wife. And what about Charlie? He'd go through hell at school, taunted by the other children.

'Oh, why did this have to happen to

me?' she moaned.

It was lucky for Maudie that she had Charlie and Rover to see to. With a lively toddler and a hungry dog vying for her attention she couldn't shrivel up and withdraw into herself. She had to prepare meals for the baby, rinse out small food-stained garments and climb up and down stairs following Charlie's daily routine.

Both the baby and Rover were restless, but taking them for a walk was out of the question. Once or twice she had to let the dog out into the garden, but she dared not show her face outside for more than the few seconds it took.

She tried to lose herself in the comfort of a favourite book, but the words seemed to dance on the page and made no sense. She was afraid to turn on the wireless in case there was something on it about the Llandyfan murder. The day dragged on.

* * *

She awoke suddenly in the night. Was that a sound? Old houses did tend to creak and groan at times but this sounded more like . . . footsteps. She froze. Someone was in the house. Had the killer come to silence her? Why hadn't Rover barked? Was the dog even now lying dead in a pool of his own blood? She shuddered at the thought.

The footsteps were coming up the stairs now. She was tempted to dive under the bed but Charlie was alone in his room, and she had to protect him, or die in the attempt. Desperately searching for a weapon in the moonlit room she snatched up the only thing she could find, a large painting of sheep in a snowy landscape, encased in a heavy frame, that had been leaning against the wall. What she intended to do with it she could never have explained; she only knew that she would never go down without a fight.

The door creaked open. Dazzled by a torch shining in her face, she choked back a cry of alarm. The intruder spoke.

'Maudie Bryant! What on earth are you doing with that picture at this time of night? And in the dark, too. You didn't intend to crown me with it, I hope.'

'Dick! Oh, Dick!' She flew into his arms, trembling with fear and relief. 'You nearly gave me a heart attack! What were you doing, creeping around in the dark like that? I thought someone had come to kill me.'

'I wasn't creeping around, as you put it. I was being careful not to wake you or the baby, that's all. It's two o'clock in the morning, in case you haven't noticed. Now let me put this picture back against the wall before somebody trips over it, and then I'll go and make us both a nice cup of tea. Just slip back into bed and I'll be back in a minute and we can catch up on all our news.'

But Maudie, unexpectedly reunited with Dick, was not about to let him out of her sight. Snatching up her dressing gown she followed him down the stairs.

'Have you had anything to eat?'

'I had something on the train, but that was hours ago. Actually I could murder a bacon sandwich.'

'I'll make us one each.' Maudie realized that she hadn't eaten all day and she was ravenously hungry now.

'How on earth did you manage to get here at this time of night?' she wondered, when the rashers were sizzling in the pan.

'The chief met me off the train and drove me here. Didn't you hear the car?'

'No.'

'Well, he did. He's been very good about all this, Maudie. He tracked me down in Scotland and gave me leave to come home. He knew you'd need me here. I just managed to catch the train by the skin of my teeth, otherwise I wouldn't have made it home for another twenty-four hours.'

'Bob thinks I did it, Dick. Murdered Verity Bourne. He came here with a constable I've never seen before, and a policewoman. At first I thought they'd come to tell me that something had happened to you, and then when they said you were all right I was afraid they were going to arrest me. I was frantic to know what would happen to Charlie if they took me away!'

'Maudie. Stop this. Listen to me. Of course Bob doesn't think you did it, but he's got to follow up every avenue, every clue, before the trail goes cold. He especially can't be seen to be partisan, or he could be accused of ignoring evidence because your husband happens to be one of his own men.'

'I suppose so.'

'And naturally I can't be involved in the investigation in any way, so you'll be glad to hear that as of now I'm on leave, with full pay. Whatever may happen next I can be at your side, old girl; every step of the way.'

Maudie's eyes filled with tears. 'Really?'

He grinned. 'I am your liege man of life and limb.'

She punched him lightly on the arm. 'Now you're teasing me, Dick Bryant!'

'Better than bawling. Things may look bleak now, but we'll get through this together. Now we should go up and get a few hours' kip. The next thing we know the nipper will be awake and we'll have to sit up and pay attention, whether we like it or not. We can talk about all this in the morning.'

So curled up against her husband's broad back, taking comfort in his nearness in their double bed, Maudie felt considerably more at peace than she had done less than an hour ago.

Whatever the coming days might bring was as much of a conundrum to her now as was the mystery of who had strangled Verity Bourne, and why they had done it. But now that Dick was home she could discuss her doubts and fears with him and that was worth a great deal. It was even possible that he possessed some vital snippet of information about the woman that would assist the police in building a picture of her background. As it happened he had spent more time talking to her than Maudie had; who knew what clues she might have let slip?

In the next room Charlie gave a little wail. Maudie stiffened, listening, but then all was quiet again, so perhaps he had only cried out in his sleep. There was no need for her to get up. She reflected that they had had quite a time with Charlie recently, as he had reached his second birthday, and there were moments when he had severely tried her patience. Now she was thankful that he was the age he was. He would come through his mother's troubles unscathed, having no understanding of what she was going through. He couldn't read newspapers, he wasn't allowed to pick up the telephone and if it came to a point where people called insults after her in the street he would have no idea what it was all about.

His father was here; honest, stalwart Dick, who would protect them both. She cuddled closer to her liege lord, and slept.

18

Having just fed Charlie, Maudie was on her second cup of tea when a knock came at the door. Alarmed, she shrank back in her chair, leaving it to Dick to see who was there at that hour of the day.

'It's Mrs Blunt!' he announced, ushering their friend into the kitchen.

'I'm so sorry not to have come before now,' Joan said, holding out a posy of pink and purple asters. 'We've been away and I've only just heard about poor Miss Bourne. The news came with the milkman. You know how he can never resist passing on gossip.'

'I do indeed,' Maudie agreed. 'Have you been away on holiday?'

'I wish we had! No, Harold was called to the deathbed of a former parishioner down in Devon, and I thought I'd go with him to share the driving. I knew Perkin would be all right on his own for a few days. He's got his cat flap and I left out plenty of dry food in his bowl, not that the wretched animal deigned to touch it! I found the remains of a squirrel on my bed when we arrived home, so obviously he's had no trouble fending for himself!'

'Ugh! Rover loves to roll in horrid things, but at least he doesn't drag them home!'

'That's the difference between a dog and a cat, I suppose. Now, I mustn't keep you. I just wanted to pop round for a minute to see how you are both bearing up.'

'Are you sure you won't stay for a cup of tea?'

'No, thanks: I must dash. Harold hasn't had his breakfast yet, and unlike Perkin he's not very good at fending for himself!' She smiled and left for home, leaving Maudie feeling much more cheerful.

'After breakfast we are going for a walk,' Dick said. 'The sun is shining and that dog needs a run. He's getting lazy and he's starting to put on weight.'

'Dick, no! I can't possibly!'

'What's the matter, old girl; afraid to show your face?'

'It's not that.'

'Oh? Then what is it, then?'

Maudie hung her head. 'I don't want people to look at me.'

'Innocent people have nothing to fear, and I know you are innocent, Maudie.'

'I bet everyone doesn't believe that.'

'Nonsense. If we stay holed up in here it will only add fuel to the fire. We'll give the boys a nice outing and while we're about it we'll call in at the village shop and catch up on all the news.'

'What if we run into a newspaper reporter on the way?'

'Then I'll send him away with a flea in his ear. Now you can jolly well stop throwing up objections, Maudie Bryant, because I'm taking you out if I have to drag you by the hair!'

There was no arguing with Dick in this mood, so Maudie reluctantly went to fetch a cardigan and her walking shoes, and they set off up the village street with Charlie riding on Dick's shoulders.

They met nobody on the road, but when they came to the shop it was hard to get inside the door because half the village seemed to have congregated there. Two women who had been standing at the counter, holding string bags bulging with tinned goods, lowered their eyes and scuttled out. Several more people followed, empty-handed.

Maudie didn't recognize them as anyone she knew well, but they obviously knew who she was, and she was persona non grata! 'What did I tell you?' she muttered.

Dick stepped up to the counter. 'I'll have a quarter of TyPhoo, please, Mrs Hatch. That's if you're willing to serve us now we've chased away all your other customers.'

'Certainly, Mr Bryant. And may I say that I totally believe in your wife's innocence, even if there are some as says otherwise.'

'That is good to know, Mrs Hatch, especially when Maudie has served this community so well for all these years. As for your less loyal customers, just what are they saying, exactly?'

'Well, I hardly like to say, Mr Bryant.'

Maudie could stand no more of this

skirting around the issue. 'Oh, you may as well spit it out, Mrs Hatch, or somebody else will. Some of them think I did it, don't they?'

The postmistress looked even more uncomfortable than before. 'It's just that everyone knows there was bad blood between you and the teacher, and now she's turned up dead . . . '

'I wasn't the only one who had a grievance against her, Mrs Hatch. Half the mothers with children in her class were up in arms. In fact they asked me to do something about it on their behalf! And no, I didn't bump her off while I was about it. I went and spoke to the vicar about it, and that was all. He was the one who went and had words with her. Why does nobody suspect him?'

'Two women were walking past your cottage the other day when they heard the pair of you yelling at each other at the top of your lungs. Naturally they felt it their duty to report what they heard when the police came asking questions. But there's more to it than that, Nurse. Miss Bourne was strangled with the belt off your dress, and that puts a different complexion on it.'

Maudie directed an angry look at Dick. Why wasn't he saying something in her defence? But he simply held his finger to his lips briefly, before shifting Charlie onto his other hip.

'How do people know about my belt?' she asked.

'Because Bart Fellowes saw it round her neck, of course. He's the bloke who found the body,' she explained, turning to Dick, as if he didn't know. 'He's been telling the world every detail ever since he found her. Of course he's doing well out of it at the Spread Eagle. People keep buying him drinks to get him to talk.'

'That's all very well, but what gave him the idea that the belt had anything to do with me?'

Mrs Hatch's face turned an unbecoming crimson. 'Well now, that might have been something to do with me. 'Looks like she was done in by one of them spotted handkerchiefs,' he says, 'only thinner, and longer. Red, with big white spots.'

' 'That sounds like Nurse Bryant's summer frock,' I says, before I stopped to think, like. 'That's got a narrow tie belt at the waist, made from the same material to match the dress.'

' 'That's right,' old Gamma Pearson says. 'She had that on when she come to the church fete, and she wore it again come Harvest Festival.''

'Well thank you very much, the lot of you!' Maudie's tone was bitter. 'Pay for that tea, Dick, and we'll go home.

'And you're just as bad, Dick Bryant!' she snapped when they were out on the street once more. 'I didn't hear you speaking up for me. That coven of witches can say what they like; is that it?'

'Simmer down, old girl. Don't you see it's better to get these things out in the open rather than letting them fester in the dark? As long as people are still talking about the murder something useful may slip out; something that will work in your favour. Besides, when this is all over the old hags will have to eat their words, and revenge will be sweet, won't it?'

'I suppose so. If it ever *is* over, which

I'm beginning to doubt!'

'Of course it will be. Now then, after lunch, when Charlie goes down for his nap, we'll look at this business properly, and see if we can come up with any rational ideas. Clues, theories, you name it. I may be officially barred from the case but I know Bob Goodman will be willing to listen to anything I can put forward.'

'All right, if you think it will help, although I can assure you that I've already racked my brains until I'm cross-eyed without coming up with anything useful. Verity Bourne was a difficult person and you were a chump to be taken in by her, but that still isn't a motive for murder.'

'I was not taken in by her, as you put it. I was only being polite to the wretched woman, as I hope I would be to any lady.'

'You and the vicar, both,' she muttered.

'The vicar? What does he have to do with anything?'

But answer came there none, as the author Lewis Carroll might have said. Much like Alice when she went through the looking glass, Maudie was experiencing a different and confusing world. Dick gave up the struggle for the time being. He knew that his wife was suffering under the most ghastly stress and there was no point in making matters worse.

19

'Right, Maudie. Let's get started.' Dick sat at the table, equipped with a notebook and pencil. 'First of all, do you have any sort of alibi for the day she died?'

'That was the morning you telephoned me. Will that do?'

'Not really. For one thing I'm your husband. Any prosecution barrister would say that I can't be trusted to speak the truth, or at least not in this instance. What we really need is a witness to say that you were somewhere else at the time of death, preferably somewhere far away. You didn't happen to take the bus to Midvale to have a look at the shops, for instance?' Maudie shook her head.

'Or go to spend time with Joan Blunt, as you sometimes do?'

'You heard what Joan said. They'd gone to Devon, that's why Bart Fellowes couldn't get into the house to call 999 and he had to do it at the shop.'

'Did you perhaps go to the village shop at any time during the day?'

Maudie shook her head again. 'Not until that woman came and fetched me. I keep telling you, Dick! While you were gone I just let everything go and gave myself a little holiday. Apart from looking after Charlie I lazed around all the time, reading and listening to the wireless.'

'But did anyone come to the door at all? Think, Maudie! Someone collecting for charity, let's say, or asking for directions?' Again she shook her head.

'What about anyone who might have been passing by the house when you were out in the garden?'

'I didn't even step outside earlier that day. Charlie spilled orange juice down his front at breakfast and I remember that had to rinse his rompers through, but it looked like it might come to rain so I hung them in the scullery. Honestly, Dick, this is quite hopeless. I saw nobody that day, and nobody saw me. Until, as I've said, I was called out to go to the shop.'

'Never mind. It was only a thought.'

Maudie sniffed. 'Even if I had been

seen around the place I can't see how that would have helped. The glebe is just the other side of the church. I could have nipped up there, strangled my nemesis, and come back home, as cool as a cucumber, to show myself to anyone who passed by on the street. Perhaps I did!'

'Don't say things like that, Maudie!'

'Why not? That's what the prosecution will say at the trial, isn't it, or something very like it.'

'It won't come to that, but if you don't take this seriously life could become very unpleasant over the next few weeks. Now for the important bit. What was your belt — that tie thing, or whatever you call it — doing up at the glebe? Had you been walking up there recently, wearing that dress? Could it have fallen off without your noticing?'

'No, to both questions. First of all, surely you know how hummocky the ground is there. They don't mow it unless it's about to be used for some official function. You should try pushing a pram over that rough grass! And it's not as if the way through the glebe leads anywhere, except to the prefabs. I've no reason to go there. And if I did, I certainly wouldn't be wearing my red dress!'

Dick frowned. 'Why not?'

'Because I keep it for best, silly! And I always wear sandals or high heels with it, not plimsolls or walking shoes.'

'But I seem to recall your wearing it to the church fete, and that was in the glebe.'

'That was months ago. Are you suggesting that my belt fell off when I was trying my luck at the hoopla stall and it's been there ever since, just waiting for a killer to strangle somebody with? No, I don't think that the belt used by the murderer is mine at all. That dress isn't unique, you know. I bought it in Marks & Spencer. There must be dozens like it.'

'Granted, but in that case why is yours missing? If you can produce it we'll be home free.'

Maudie shrugged. 'I've had that frock out a couple of times recently, trying to see if it's possible to let it out a bit in the bodice. The belt might have fallen off and been picked up by Rover, or Charlie; you know how they like dangling things. Or for all I know it never came home after the last time it went to the dry cleaner's.' That was unlikely, however, because the cleaners always made sure that loose bits were attached to the main garment with a safety pin before being handed back over the counter.

'Let's try a different tack, Maudie. What was Miss Bourne doing in the glebe in the middle of a school day? It's quite some distance from the school if she only needed a breath of fresh air.'

'How should I know? She's new here, so perhaps she wanted to look at the place to see if it was suitable for some school event.'

'What sort of event? They hold the sports day in the summer term, don't they?'

'So she must have been lured there, then.'

'By whom?'

'Really, Dick! Be your age! By the murderer, of course. He wanted to bump her off so he chose a time when all the local kids would be at school, and he

171

wouldn't be noticed about the place.'

'I must admit that sounds as likely as anything we've come up with so far, but who could it be? And the motive?'

'An outsider, Dick. Some chap who followed her down from Newcastle, or wherever it is she came from. Go and ask the vicar, or Cora Beasley, where Verity was teaching last year. Enquiries can be made up there.'

'You forget that I'm not on the case.'

'No, but you can let Bob Goodman know.'

Dick stood up, stretching. 'I need to clear my head. You don't mind if I go out for a stroll, do you?'

'Of course not. I think I'll just read for a bit. See you later.'

★ ★ ★

But Maudie's thoughts were in a whirl and she couldn't settle down. She kept thinking about that narrow tie belt, and suddenly it came back to her. How on earth could she have forgotten, when this was so important to her? The last time she'd had the dress out Charlie had reached up to the table and pulled the belt down. The dog had joined in the fun, taking the belt in his teeth to worry it in play. Charlie had clung to his end, chuckling away. Maudie had taken it from them and put it further back on the table, out of reach.

She caught her breath as memories continued to come flooding back. That was the day when Verity had burst into the cottage, enraged because she'd received a reprimand from the vicar. She had stood beside the table to deliver her rant. She could well have taken the belt, but it was stupid to think so. Why would she have wanted to? And why would it have been so conveniently to hand when somebody wanted to throttle her?

Now a new thought hit Maudie. Jerry Saunders had arrived immediately afterwards, and he'd sat down at the table and even admired the dress. She had put it on the sideboard when she'd brought the tea things the table, but she hadn't paid much attention and the belt could have been gone.

She drew her breath in sharply. Jerry had shown concern that Verity was being difficult. Hadn't he said that he didn't like to think of Maudie being bothered by her? Had he stolen the belt, stalked Verity and killed her, using her victim's belt as the final irony?

No, it wasn't possible. Not gentle Jerry! Yet this was not the same man she remembered from her youth. His terrible experiences in captivity, the sights he had seen and the deaths of so many of his friends, had by his own admission affected him badly. He was a bundle of nerves. What if . . . '

Maudie sat with her head in her hands, feeling sick. By his own admission Jerry still 'carried a torch' for his boyhood sweetheart. While in prison camp he'd had to stand by while unspeakable things were done to other prisoners, atrocities he was powerless to prevent. Had he now seen Maudie in a spot of difficulty and come to the rescue like St George of old, slaying a dragon in order to save the life of a helpless maiden? Of course no possible comparison could be made between the dark deeds of wartime and the little bit of fuss and bother Maudie was having with the school teacher, but would that mean anything to poor Jerry, if his brain had been turned, making him mentally ill? And if Jerry was found guilty he would be hanged, or be kept in a mental asylum for the rest of his days, and she couldn't bear to think of that.

The back door slammed, heralding Dick's return.

'Dick,' she called, 'can you come in here? I have something to tell you.'

20

'I think I know how it may have happened,' Maudie said. 'What I mean is, how my belt got out of the house. When it did. Or if it did.'

Dick frowned. 'Stop babbling, old girl. You're not making any sense.'

'I told you how Jerry Saunders dropped in while you were away? You didn't mind, did you? We do go back a long way and we hadn't seen each other for years. I couldn't very well tell him to go away when he turned up on the doorstep.'

'Go on.'

'Well, as I told you before, my dress was on the table at the time. I'd put it down to answer the door when Verity showed up. It was still there when I let Jerry in.'

'And was he left alone with it at any time? When you went to see to Charlie, let's say?'

'I did go to the kitchen to make us a

cup of tea. I was gone for all of five minutes.'

'And did the frock look any different when you returned?'

Maudie shrugged. 'How should I know? I put the tray down on the table while I picked up the dress and put it on the sideboard. Then I came back and poured the tea. And before you ask, no, I didn't notice if the belt was gone. Why should I? The dress was all of a heap, not folded or anything.'

Dick ran a finger across his lower lip. 'It isn't much to go on, but it's something, I suppose. If your Jerry took it that could at least explain how it got out of the house, putting you in the clear.'

'He's not my Jerry, Dick!'

'Just a figure of speech, love. So you go to make the tea, he sees his chance, he whips the belt off the table and crams it into his pocket. You come back with the tray, move the frock to the sideboard, and Bob's your uncle.'

'That's what it looks like,' she admitted.

'But why take your belt, and what did

he mean to do with it; that's the question. He couldn't have planned to kill Verity Bourne; he didn't even know her. Or did he decide to take it just in case he needed to strangle someone?'

'Dick Bryant! This is no joking matter!'

'Indeed it is not,' he agreed. 'I don't know what this means, but the chief needs to hear about it. I'll give him a ring right away.'

Poor Maudie was consumed by guilt. It grieved her to think that she'd landed Jerry in trouble; poor Jerry who had survived life as a POW by living on boyhood memories of her. And now she had planted the idea in Dick's brain that Jerry might have killed Verity Bourne in some mad impulse to avenge her unkind treatment of Maudie! Verity might have been a nasty piece of work, but you don't kill someone just because she has a spiteful nature.

No, said the little voice in Maudie's head. No sane person would dream of doing such a thing, unless they were driven to it in a moment of fury, which was unlikely in the case of Jerry, who seemed totally lacking in energy. But was Jerry totally sane? After the atrocities he'd witnessed in POW camp, had he been left with a burning desire to see justice done, whenever his world seemed out of shape?

'All done and dusted!' Dick announced, coming back to the sitting room. 'The chief will put somebody on it right away. In the meantime I think we can do a bit of snooping around on our own, don't you?'

Maudie brightened. 'I thought you were supposed to steer clear of the investigation.'

'Let's put it this way. You've been cooped up here long enough. I'll take you out to lunch at the Spread Eagle. If I happen to have a bit of a natter with the landlord, where's the harm in that? He must have formed some sort of opinion of Saunders when the chap stayed there.'

This was more like it. A pub lunch was just what she needed. The landlord kept a high chair handy just in case people like themselves popped in with a toddler in tow, so there was no problem about getting Charlie looked after while his parents went on their fact-finding mission. She would take some arrowroot biscuits with her in a paper bag and with any luck that would keep him quiet until they were ready to leave.

* * *

The Spread Eagle was an ancient hostelry dating back to the stage coach days. The public bar, shrouded in cigarette smoke, would not have done for Charlie at all, but meals were served in a separate little room adjoining the kitchen. It wasn't as smart as the Copper Kettle, the room that the local ladies preferred, but it was homely and clean, and Dora Frost's cooking was more than adequate.

Maudie ordered a chicken salad, regretfully turning down the idea of anything fattening. Dick opted for the ploughman's lunch: a doorstep of crusty bread, a large wedge of mousetrap cheese and a pickled onion.

'And don't you dare breathe on me after eating that thing!' she told him. 'You know how I hate onion breath!'

'If you'd have one yourself there

wouldn't be any problem,' he told her, biting into the onion so that it squelched and sent pickle juice flying in an arc over the table. Maudie tutted and moved her chair aside.

'Anyone for afters?' Dora asked, poking her head round the kitchen door. 'I've a lovely rhubarb crumble, and lashings of cream to go with it!'

Dick's eyes lit up. 'I'll have a double helping, please!'

'Right-ho. How about you, Mrs Bryant?'

'No, thanks,' said Maudie, primly. 'And as for you, Dick Bryant, what on earth do you think you're doing? Rhubarb, on top of pickled onions? Don't blame me if you're up all night with the collywobbles.'

'A man must be master in his own home, old girl. That's right, Mrs Frost; a double helping, please.'

'I don't know what that's supposed to mean,' Maudie muttered. 'You're not in your own home now!'

'Maybe not, but the principle's the same, and don't you forget it!' They continued to bicker in a friendly fashion, with Charlie joining in the fun by banging on his table with a spoon. Anyone who happened to watching the trio would have reckoned them to be a happy little family without a care in the world, enjoying a pleasant outing, but then appearances can so often be deceptive.

* * *

When the lunchtime rush had died down Dick went to speak to the landlord while Maudie took Charlie outside, to sit with the waiting Rover.

'I can't say I formed much of an impression about the chap,' Len Frost muttered, polishing glasses as he spoke. 'He hadn't much to say for himself, except when he noticed that picture of your missus on the wall up there.' He waved at the framed clipping with his tea towel.

'And how did he react, I wonder?'

'Why, he got all excited. Wanted to know if that was his Maudie, someone he'd known before the war.

' "That's Nurse Bryant,' we told him. 'Lives just round the corner, she does.'

' 'She wasn't Bryant when I knew her,' he says, 'but I'm sure that's her. She went away to work as a nurse so it must be the same girl. To think that I've found her again, after all this time. I can't believe it!' '

'And was that all?'

'Pretty much.'

Dick drummed his fingers on the bar counter. 'I was hoping for something more.'

'Like what?'

'That's just the trouble; I don't know. I suppose he signed the register, seeing as he stayed here with you? Can I have a look?'

'Be my guest.' Frost lifted the flap that gave access to the working side of the bar, and led the way to the deserted little hall beyond the public side of the building.

Sadly, the register didn't tell him any more than he knew already. A tight little signature gave the name G. H. Saunders and for a moment Dick puzzled over that, until he realized that Jerry must be short for Gerald, hence the discrepancy. The address given was not that of a private residence, but a firm of stationers, apparently the man's employers. Oh, well, they should be easy enough to trace, and from there the police could find out where Maudie's old friend was staying, and put him through the wringer if necessary.

During his brief meeting with the man Dick had formed the impression of a quiet, nervous sort of chap, one who was hardly likely to go round strangling women. But then, as he well knew, some of the most unlikely people turned out to be murderers. For old times' sake Maudie could be as protective of the fellow as she liked, but Dick was a police officer, and made of sterner stuff. If this man had killed Verity Bourne, and left Maudie to take the blame, Dick would show him no mercy.

21

Joan Blunt arrived, bearing gifts. One pot of greengage jam, homemade. A small cake tin which, opened, revealed a layer of melting moments.

'Lovely!' said Dick, putting one of the soft biscuits in his mouth after looking longingly at the jam.

'This is very good of you,' Maudie said, relishing the display of friendship shown as much as the actual gifts. 'You didn't need to go to all this trouble. The jam would have been quite enough.'

'I was making the biscuits anyway,' Mrs Blunt said. 'Harold is very partial to a melting moment but they're so fiddly to make, and then you have to wash out the beastly piping bag. So I thought I might as well be hung for a sheep as a lamb, and make a double batch.'

'And much appreciated they are, too,' Dick said, reaching for another and getting his hand slapped by Maudie.

'Anyway, I just thought I'd pop round to see how you are.'

'As well as can be expected,' Dick said. 'Maudie hasn't been charged with anything, and it's unlikely that she will be, but she's already been judged by some of the locals, and that's pretty hard to swallow.'

'Of course it is, and I know that Harold wishes he could do something about it. I heard him muttering to himself this morning, 'For thus saith the Lord, Behold, I will make thee a terror to thyself and to all thy friends: and they shall fall by the sword of their enemies, and thine eyes shall behold it.''

'I assume that's a quotation from the Good Book,' Dick remarked.

'Jeremiah.'

'It would be. I must say it fits the situation, Mrs Blunt. A few people round here will have to eat their words when we get to the bottom of this dreadful business.'

'They will soon have other things to talk about. Did you know that a temporary replacement has been found for poor

Miss Bourne at the school? A Mrs Lucy Snead, from the prefabs.'

'Really? I don't think I know her,' Maudie said.

'No, perhaps you wouldn't. She's a retired teacher in her early seventies, recently arrived from Liverpool. Her husband passed away a couple of years ago and she's come to Llandyfan to be near her married daughter and grandchildren.'

'That's nice. Will she be able to manage the pupils, at her age?'

'I understand she's in good health and eager to get to know people in the community. Harold went to speak to her last evening and she agreed at once. I know it seems callous to be replacing Miss Bourne so soon after her death, but Miss Rice really can't be expected to manage the whole school by herself. She has enough on her plate with Standards four to six without trying to deal with tearful newcomers as well.'

'Not to mention Eddie Lunney,' Maudie murmured.

'And talking about Eddie Lunney, have you seen what his mother has done to her hair? Singed it with the curling tongs by the look of it and now her fringe looks a bit moth-eaten.'

'I think that if nobody needs me for anything I'll just go out and have a look at my garden,' Dick said, standing up. The two women ignored him.

'She's the daughter of that Mrs Polley I met recently, isn't she?' Maudie said. 'Isn't her husband supposed to be coming home from sea soon? I suppose she wants to pretty herself up for him and she can't afford to go to the hairdresser.'

'Much good it will do her, poor soul. He's here already, but I gather from Dora Frost that he's hardly ever out of the Spread Eagle. At one point she asked him if he'd like her to make him a sandwich to soak up some of the ale he's been pouring down his throat, but he told her to mind her own business or he'd take his custom elsewhere. Not that he was as polite as that! Apparently he treated her to a lot of seaman's curses and Len had to step in and warn him to watch his language.'

'Perhaps that's where young Eddie gets it from. Bullying, I mean.'

'Perhaps so, Nurse, although the older I get the more I tend to believe in Original Sin. I think that some people are born with a tendency towards a life of crime and society can never do much to reform them.'

'The old question,' Maudie agreed. 'Nature versus nurture.'

'Just so. I mean, prison is supposed to reform criminals, isn't that right? But every day we read in the newspapers about some recently released con man who has been caught reoffending, and back he goes for another stretch behind bars.'

'And do you think we have a case of that here? A convicted killer just out of prison has come looking for another victim, and Miss Bourne just happened to cross his path?'

'That's not very likely when we have the death penalty, Nurse. He'd have gone to the gallows the first time, wouldn't he? But I can't stay here all day gossiping, pleasant though it has been! I must get home and see about Harold's lunch. But don't you worry; right is on your side. DI Goodman and his men will soon sort this business out, and I know they'll make an extra effort because you are Mr Bryant's wife.'

'I hope so. But it's so hard, waiting and wondering.'

'Of course it is, but you must have faith. Goodbye, my dear. I'll call round again soon.'

★   ★   ★

'Has she gone?' Dick peered round the kitchen door, not wanting to tramp over the living room carpet in his muddy boots.

'Yes, she's just left.'

'Then hadn't you better get lunch started?'

'Why? What's the big rush?'

'It's Wednesday. You and the nipper have your mum and baby thing.'

'I'm a bit tired. I think I'll give it a miss today. Somebody else can lead *Pop Goes the Weasel.*'

'Afraid to show your face, aren't you!'

'That's not very kind, Dick Bryant!' Maudie hurled a cushion at him and missed. Surprised out of a sound sleep, Rover yelped and shot behind the settee.

'Maybe, maybe not, but you've got to keep a stiff upper lip, my girl. You put your glad rags on and hop on over to the parish hall. Let them see what's what. You've nothing to be ashamed of and I want you to let the whole world know it.'

'I might.'

'Of course you will. Would you like me to give you a police escort?'

Maudie grinned. 'Oh, I think I can manage on my own, thank you very much. But if I'm to get my strength up I really should rest a while longer before I go. Perhaps you could make the dinner instead? There are sausages in the larder or you could open a tin of spam. And how about some of your very own homegrown spuds to go with it?'

'Don't press your luck!' Dick growled, in mock warning. Maudie laughed.

* * *

And so, holding an exuberant Charlie, she entered the parish hall, sick at heart but determined to keep the flag flying. She noticed at once that the numbers were down, but possibly that was only to be expected. One or two women avoided her eye but on the plus side a plump pre-schooler shyly handed her a posy of michaelmas daisies, while her mother smiled encouragement from her chair.

Then a little boy toddled up with a crayoned drawing to show her, and another young mother took Charlie by the hand and enticed him into a game of *Ring O' Roses*. 'All fall down!' he shouted with the best of them. Collapsing on his well-padded bottom was something he was very good at.

Stirring herself to action Maudie started a game of *Oranges and Lemons*. The words of the song were beyond the capabilities of most of the children but their mothers remembered the game from their own childhood and joined in lustily while their youngsters marched around the room in a wavering line. 'Here comes a candle to light you to bed . . . ' and then squeals of mock terror as the last man was caught trying to get through the arch made by two women holding their arms aloft.

Little by little her spirits rose. Dick had been right, of course. She'd been wise to show her face, and an afternoon spent with innocent children had been just what she needed to help restore her peace of mind.

22

Dick, out for a stroll with Rover, stopped to look into the window of the village shop, where Mrs Hatch had built a pyramid of tinned fruit. Next time Maudie came shopping he must ask her to buy a tin of those peaches. They were especially good with evaporated milk and he wasn't given them as often as he'd like. His wife was always saying he should eat more fruit and less stodge, wasn't she?

Mrs Hatch opened the door, waving a newspaper at him. 'You should see this, Mr Bryant; you should, really.'

Dick fumbled in his trouser pocket for loose change but found nothing there but a stray ha'penny. 'Sorry, Mrs Hatch. I seem to have come out without any money. Is there something interesting in the paper?'

'Here, take it. On the house!' She thrust it at him and disappeared back inside.

That was odd. The postmistress was

kindly enough in her way, but where her profits were concerned she ran a tight ship. Since when had she started giving newspapers away? Besides, the *Daily Express* had already been delivered to the house before school that morning, pushed through the letterbox by a spotty youth called Damien. What could there possibly be in this tabloid that hadn't been picked up by the *Express*?'

Opening the paper he soon found out. A blurry picture of Verity Bourne was splashed across two columns, with the caption *Teacher murdered in Llandyfan. Inhabitants in state of terror. See page four.*

'I'll give them state of terror!' Dick muttered, ignoring his dog who jumped up against him, adding another layer of mud to his gardening trousers. 'How did they get this story up in London, anyway? And aren't they a bit late? The woman's been dead for days.'

He turned to page four and cursed. The photo there showed his own cottage, with Charlie peering through the garden gate. Since this trouble started they hadn't let the boy play outside alone, so either Maudie or Dick himself must have been loitering somewhere in the background. Fortunately neither of them had been snapped. A line of washing suggested that Maudie had been pegging things out and had just gone back inside to fetch another load of sheets.

'What brings you back so soon?' Maudie looked up from the sock she was darning. 'I thought you were going to walk up to the football ground.'

'Mrs Hatch gave me this. I think you'd better have a look.'

'*The Daily Pilot*? She's made a mistake. We've never taken that rag.'

'Better take a look.'

'Can't you read it to me? You can see I'm busy. My sewing basket is overflowing and if I don't get busy soon you'll have to go back to a work with a potato in your foot, as my Grandma used to say.'

Dick sat down and began to read aloud. 'Once again the small village of Llandyfan is fair set to win the title of murder capital of rural England. The murder by strangulation of schoolmistress

Verity Bourne is the latest in a string of killings involving midwife Monica Bryant, wife of the village constable.'

'Well, what a cheek!' cried Maudie, stabbing her darning needle into the sock and narrowly missing her hand in the process. 'They make it sound as if I'm bumping people off all over the place and they can't even get my name right! And how dare they call you the village constable? You're a Detective Sergeant now. I suppose we're lucky they realized Llandyfan is in England, even if it does have a Welsh name.'

'I'm afraid there's worse, old girl.'

'Get on with it, then.'

'The unfortunate Miss Bourne was strangled with the belt of a summer frock allegedly owned by Nurse Bryant. Several of the local ladies confirm that the midwife does indeed own such a garment that is bright red with an overall pattern of large white spots.

'Our reporter spoke with Mr Bartholomew Fellowes, who provided a graphic description of what he had discovered on that fateful day. 'It were 'orrible. She were lying there all purple in the face like a giant plum about to burst. There was this bit of stuff round her neck, cutting into the skin. A long sort of tie thing, it was, red with white spots. I'll never forget the sight of that poor woman lying there like a dead rabbit. Whoever done it wants killing hisself. I hope they string him up high and make him suffer the way she suffered.'

'Police are close-mouthed about the case, which comes as no surprise when the suspect is married to one of their own. Sources say that the inquisitive nurse is an enthusiastic sleuth who in the past has helped the authorities to solve many a crime, but this time the gumshoe is on the other foot. Can hubby rescue her from the trouble she finds herself in, or will the judge don his black cap when it's too late to save her? We will bring you more details on this fascinating case as we receive them.'

Maudie could understand her son's frustration when at times he couldn't get his own way. She wanted to get up and shout and scream, dancing from one foot to the other like a cannibal who has just noticed that the fire has gone out underneath the cooking pot. 'Where do they get this rubbish, Dick?'

'They've made half of it up, of course. Notice they say 'allegedly' to avoid giving us grounds to sue them.'

'I'd like to get my hands on those women who described my frock!'

'I don't suppose they went running to the paper with that information. All it needed was for the reporter to ask one or two local people if they'd seen you wearing such a thing and even if they declined to answer it would be confirmation of sorts.'

'But this says I'm a suspect! How can they say that, Dick? I haven't been arrested, or even taken to Midvale to answer questions! Now the whole world thinks I'm a murdereress and I can't bear it!'

Dick moved to her side and held her while she sobbed. If he could get his hands on that reporter, he thought grimly, Verity Bourne's death wouldn't be the only case of strangulation on the books!

23

Once again Maudie was invited to a tea party at Cora Beasley's home. 'Just the four of us, Nurse; you, me, Mrs Blunt and Lucy Snead, the new substitute teacher. I thought it would be nice to welcome Mrs Snead, not only to the district but to the school family. I would of course have invited Miss Rice as well, but naturally she is tied up at school in the afternoons.'

'I'm sure you could decree a half holiday,' Maudie said, only half joking. She could well remember from her own schooldays the visit of a governor announcing a holiday, which was greeted with cheers and screams of delight.

'The children would like that, I'm sure, but this is a purely social occasion and since Miss Rice has already met with Mrs Snead, closing the school is hardly justified. Besides, there has been enough disruption already.'

'Just a thought!' Maudie knew that the partition that separated the infants' room from that of the older children would have been rolled back to enable Miss Rice to deal with all six classes at once. A sobering thought, but she had no doubt that the headmistress could cope.

'Of course I'd like to go to this tea party,' Maudie told Dick, 'but why me? It's not as if I'm the school nurse any more, and Charlie won't be one of her pupils.'

'You've been an important personage in the area for years, old girl. Just think, you've probably brought every one of her prospective pupils into this world. Why wouldn't she want to meet you?' Privately Dick thought that Mrs Beasley had only invited Maudie as a way to show solidarity but he did not voice the thought. His wife's self-esteem had suffered enough in recent weeks without any putdowns from him.

★　★　★

Maudie took an immediate liking to Lucy Snead. A no-nonsense grandmotherly type, she was dressed in a plain pink cotton blouse and a blue tweed skirt, sagging at the seat. Her white hair showed signs of having received a recent perm; when the curls loosened a little they would frame her lined face like a halo. Her voice was low and clear, her manner decisive and firm. On the basis of this first meeting it appeared that she would make an ideal teacher for the tinies at Llandyfan School.

'How are you enjoying your retirement?' Mrs Blunt asked, getting the conversational ball rolling.

'Not as much as I thought I might,' the teacher said, with a rueful smile. 'It's lovely for me to have my daughter and my grandchildren close by, but I had to leave all my friends behind which was a blow. I've tried to fill the gap by taking up water-colour painting, and I've lost count of the garments I've knitted for refugees, but it's not the same as having a good old natter with a chum, is it? Those prefabs are rather small and sometimes I fancy I can feel the walls closing in. Still, I mustn't grumble! I was lucky to get one at all.'

'You'll soon make friends here,' Joan Blunt said. 'You must join the Mother's Union or the W. I., mustn't she, Mrs Beasley?'

'Certainly you must, and I advise you not to let slip that you find yourself at a loose end, or you'll find yourself serving on a dozen different committees before you have time to turn around! That happened to me after my husband passed away, and now I never seem to have a spare moment.'

'In that case it was good of you to invite me to tea,' Mrs Snead murmured, passing her cup for a refill. She turned to Maudie. 'And I understand that you are retired as well, Mrs Bryant. Do you miss nursing?'

'I do, in a way, although I can't say that I'll never nurse again. I married rather late in life, you see, and now we have a little boy who keeps me busy. But who knows what I might decide to do after Charlie is grown up?'

'I believe you may know something about Miss Bourne's dealings at the school, Mrs Bryant. Wasn't she the subject of some controversy? Not to speak ill of the dead, of course, but I do feel I ought to know what I'm getting into. Was she as difficult as people say, or are the local children particularly unruly?'

Maudie's cheeks reddened. How was she supposed to reply to that? Surely Lucy Snead must have heard the rumours? She must have seen the newspapers, even that revolting article in the *Pilot*.

Cora Beasley came to her rescue. 'I think you'll find that Miss Rice runs a well-ordered school, Mrs Snead. The children's behaviour is no worse and no better than you'll find in a small village school anywhere in the kingdom. Mind you, we do have one little boy who tends to be rather over-active, isn't that so, Nurse?'

'Pardon?'

'Eddie Lunney. I was just telling Mrs Snead how his disruption resulted in trouble for Miss Bourne in the community.'

'Oh, yes. Sorry! It was when you mentioned the kingdom. It got me thinking: we have a queen now, so why don't we call it the Queendom?'

'I believe it's a general term,' Mrs Blunt said. 'Like the Kingdom of Heaven, you know?'

The talk turned to a discussion about words and expressions then and the subject of Eddie Lunney was forgotten. Had it been continued, the whole miserable episode of Maudie's involvement — or lack of it — with Verity Bourne's death might have come to an end far sooner, but life has a way of taking detours when we would prefer to travel a straight road.

* * *

'How was it?' Dick enquired when Maudie returned home, having been given a lift in the vicarage car. 'Did you have a nice time?'

'Quite pleasant, thank you. Mrs Beasley served us a delicious Victoria sponge cake, oozing with strawberry jam and whipped cream.'

'Didn't she send a piece for me?'

'No. She said she would have done, except she thinks it wouldn't be a kindness because you're fat enough already.'

'She never did!'

'Of course she didn't, you fool! I had two slices, though, so you might say I ate your piece for you.'

'So kind!'

'That Lucy Snead seems very nice, but she made me feel a bit uncomfortable when she started asking questions about Verity Bourne and the goings-on at the school. Surely she must know what has happened to me! Even if she's missed all the brouhaha in the newspapers her own daughter must have filled her in. Wouldn't you think she'd understand how this is a sore subject with me?'

'So what did you tell her?'

'Nothing. Nothing at all. Somehow we got talking about something else and that was it.'

'Perhaps I should have a word with the lady.'

'No, Dick; you don't have to do that. Really, it was something and nothing, that's all.'

'I didn't mean I was going to rush in

and tell her she can jolly well keep her questions to herself, because my wife had suffered enough! I'm well aware you can fight your own battles, old girl, if battles there be! But she's about to start at the school, and she could well turn up something that will help the investigation, and I want to ask if she'd report it to me.'

'I fail to see what she could find. Secret messages written on the blackboard? Cryptic notes in the waste paper basket? Really, Dick; aren't you clutching at straws?'

'You know very well that police work is all about keeping an open mind. Sifting through things that may make no sense at first glance but which may come to have meaning in conjunction with something else found later. Although I wasn't referring to looking for clues. The chief has already had someone going through that classroom, as well as Miss Bourne's lodgings, and as far as I know they haven't come up with anything useful.

'But in the course of her work Mrs Snead will be meeting the parents. I've no doubt that they will be keen to meet her, to discuss any problems their children might have. They may let slip something that will be useful to us and I don't intend to let the opportunity pass by. I shall go and have a word with the lady and I'm sure she'll be delighted to cooperate with the police.'

Maudie wasn't convinced. DI Goodman had already spoken to all and sundry in those vital hours and days soon after the school teacher's body was discovered. If he had learned anything useful he wasn't making it public, and if he had not, why should anything turn up now? Still, she knew better than to interfere when Dick was doing his job, and she was thankful to be married to a police detective. Some day the trail might grow cold and his colleagues would be assigned to other cases, but Dick would never give up. He would be like Rover when he found one of his master's socks discarded on the bathroom floor: he would take it in his jaws and worry it until it gave up the struggle.

24

Dick went to answer the phone. He returned to the kitchen, looking jubilant. 'That was the chief. Somebody walked into the police station at Reading and confessed to killing Verity Bourne.'

'No!' Maudie dropped the potato she was peeling. 'That's wonderful news! And why Reading? That's a long way from here.'

'It is if it's true, love. Every time there's a violent death on the news any number of nutters come forward to confess to being responsible. Heaven knows why they do it: whether it's to get a few hours in the limelight, or because they're mentally ill and controlled by mysterious voices, they rush in to put their hands up for something they've never done. We mustn't get our hopes up too soon.'

Maudie bent to retrieve the potato and stared at him. 'I can tell you're not telling me the whole story, Dick Bryant. What else is there?' Dick hesitated.

'Well, go on! Surely Bob must have told you something more than that.'

'Yes, well, the thing is, old girl, it was your old pal, Jerry Saunders.'

'Jerry? He confessed, you say?'

Dick winced at the pain in his wife's voice. 'I know it's hard to accept, but we've known all along that everything points to him. He had the motive. He had the opportunity. He had the weapon to hand, and now it seems definite that he used it to kill.'

'Not much of a motive, Dick,' Maudie whispered. 'It can't be true. There must be some mistake. I don't want it to be Jerry. I've known him since the day I was born, or at least the day when I sat up and began to take notice.'

'If you only knew how many times we've heard people say that our accusations can't be true. The family, or neighbours of someone who has committed murder or done some other awful crime. 'It simply has to be a mistake, officer. Tom wouldn't hurt a fly.' Or 'John is such a gentleman. He never would have behaved like that in a public park.' The plain fact of the matter is that the police simply do not make mistakes as often as some people like to think, and I'm not just saying that because I'm a copper myself.'

'I know.'

'But cheer up, love. Your Jerry will get a fair shake. They've already begun looking into his background, and we should hear something soon.'

★   ★   ★

Joan Blunt came to the door, bearing a small bunch of marigolds and half an apple pie. 'I've been having a pastry making day, and this is the result, or half of it. The rest of it is for our own tea. I should have had a batch of sausage rolls to share, as well, but I suppose you can guess what became of them.'

Maudie grinned. 'You left them to cool on the marble slab in the pantry and Perkin slipped in through the open window and did his worst.'

'Ten out of ten! He didn't actually get

the chance to scoff any down because he knocked the tray on the floor and I heard the crash. If it had happened during the war I might have been tempted to pick the fluff off them and serve them to my unsuspecting husband, but I couldn't bring myself to do it now. What a waste of ingredients though, and I can't even put them in the pig bin. Sausage rolls would be an insult to any self-respecting pig, don't you think?'

'I have something to tell you,' Maudie said, after they had sat in silence for a few minutes, watching Charlie playing with a bendy bunny toy which he squeezed and pummeled to the accompaniments of squeals of delight. 'Somebody has come forward and confessed to the murder of Miss Bourne.'

'Why, that's splendid, Nurse! I hope to see your name cleared in the very near future, not that anyone who knows you has believed for a moment that you had anything to do with such a horrible thing! Aren't you pleased?'

'In one way I am, Mrs Blunt.'

'And in another?'

'The man is my childhood friend, Jerry Saunders. I've told you about him.'

'Oh, my dear; that is awkward. But if he's guilty then it's best you know now, rather than wondering about it for years to come.'

'You know that Dick went to Scotland on that course having to do with the law and police work? Well, it seems that they look at crime differently there. Where our courts have a choice of two verdicts when a person is tried — innocent or guilty — they have a third option. It's called 'not proven.''

'Which means?'

'Which means that everybody thinks the person on trial is guilty all right, but they don't have enough evidence to prove it. Perhaps I'm a horrible person, Mrs Blunt, but I want somebody to pay for this crime, leaving no doubt in anyone's mind that he's the guilty party and therefore I'm completely innocent!'

'That's doesn't make you a horrible person, Nurse!'

'But don't you see? It would mean I want Jerry to hang and it doesn't matter what he's done. I can't bear the thought of it!'

* * *

Several days later Dick had more news to pass on to his wife. 'It appears that after Saunders was repatriated to Britain he spent several years in a mental institution on the south coast. His wartime experiences had been too much for his brain to handle, and he cracked.'

'A nervous breakdown, then?'

'Something like that. When nothing more could be done for him he was released, to get on with living out in the community as best he could. The psychiatrist that Bob Goodman spoke to said that Saunders wasn't thought to be a danger to himself or others and, as always, they needed the bed, as they so elegantly put it.'

'Poor Jerry.'

'At least he probably won't hang. I imagine they'll find him of unsound mind.'

'And then he'll spend the rest of his

days in a mental institution for the criminally insane. I'm not sure I wouldn't rather be dead.'

★ ★ ★

But as it turned out the case was far from over. 'Here's a turn-up for the books!' Dick said, scratching his head. 'The chief says that your friend Jerry has a cast-iron alibi for the period in which Miss Bourne was killed.'

'What!'

'He was in hospital in Winchester with a bump on his head the size of my fist! He'd been in a car accident the day before and arrived in Casualty unconscious. They thought at first that he might have a fractured skull, which turned out not to be the case, but when he came round he seemed confused so he was kept in for a few days under observation. His car was a complete wreck so as soon as they let him out he got on a train — and no, I don't know where he thought he was going — and that's when he found a copy of that ghastly newspaper abandoned on a seat and read about what had been going on here. He got off the train at Reading and went and made his confession.'

'He must have still been confused by that bump on the head and got his dates mixed up.'

'Either that or he thought the police wouldn't know about his hospital stay.'

'So he did it to save me.'

'Not necessarily. This is a man with mental difficulties, Maudie. He may have felt angry with Verity for the way she spoke to you, wished he could do something to help, and then retreated into a private fantasy world in which he believed he'd killed her.'

'Aren't we forgetting one thing? My belt! If somebody completely different killed Verity, how on earth did they get hold of that belt?'

'You must have dropped it outside at some point and someone picked it up.'

But Maudie knew quite well that she had done no such thing, and the idea of some stranger creeping into the house while she was upstairs or working in the kitchen was just too horrid. Yet she knew that she'd kept the doors locked while Dick was away, except for opening the front door to admit bona fide callers, so how could that have happened? Somewhere there had to be a missing link.

Would this nasty business never end? Just when she was beginning to think they could somehow get over this dark journey and return to their normal, everyday existence, fate shook the kaleidoscope and the pattern changed yet again.

25

Bit by bit Jerry's story became clearer. Dick wanted to keep the information from his wife but Maudie insisted on knowing every detail and he was forced to give in.

'According to my contact in the Met, Saunders has been living in a dingy bedsit in London, in a condemned building that should have been demolished long ago. The trouble is of course that the completion rate of new accommodation hasn't yet caught up with the desperate need for housing, especially in cities like London that were so badly bombed during the Blitz. People like your old friend, with few resources, have to take whatever shelter they can find. At least he hasn't been living under the arches, like some.'

Maudie's thoughts went to Jerry's widowed mother, who had slaved day and night to keep a roof over her little boy's head after his father had perished in the

Great War. Despite her poverty there had always been a slice of bread and dripping for a hungry child, and as far as she knew the rent had always been paid, right up to the end. And that same roof had disappeared in the next war, which had followed all too soon.

'Now Saunders won't be able to stay in that miserable bedsit, for he's lost his job.'

'No!'

'I'm afraid so. Apparently his sales record has been dismal and he'd been cautioned by his employer that he faced dismissal if he didn't buck up. Smashing the car was the last straw, so he's out on his ear. At least he's tucked up in a nice cosy gaol cell for a while.'

'That's cruel, Dick.'

'Just facing facts. Besides he's due to have a psychiatric assessment and it wouldn't surprise me if he's sent back to that place where he was treated after the war. Perhaps only as a voluntary patient; that will be for the medicos to decide. At least he won't have to spend the coming winter living rough.'

'Oh, Dick! Can't we get Cora Beasley

or someone to pull strings and get him into the prefabs here? I could keep an eye on him and . . . '

'No, my girl. Absolutely not! Quite apart from anything else he needs professional help, and you are a midwife, not an expert in mental disorders. And it would do him no service to become dependent on you when you couldn't possibly mother him for ever.'

'But I just want to know if he's all right. And I would like to ask him about the tie belt from my dress.'

'The chief has agreed that after Saunders gets moved down to Devon I can go and see him. Apparently he becomes quite distressed when anyone on the force tries to question him, but Bob thinks I may have better luck because I'm married to you, a link with his childhood.'

'Then I'm coming with you! Even if they won't let me inside I can walk in the grounds and he can wave to me through the window. Please, Dick! I won't take no for an answer.'

'And just what do you propose to do with Charlie?'

'We'll take him with us. And the Blunts will look after Rover.'

'I know I'm going to regret this,' Dick said.

⋆   ⋆   ⋆

However, to Maudie's great disappointment, she had to remain at home. Charlie woke up on the day of Dick's departure, grizzling and covered in sweat. 'One hundred and one!' Maudie exclaimed, when she had taken his temperature.

'What do you think is the matter with him?' Dick asked.

'I'm not sure, but there's chickenpox in the village and he's feverish. He could have picked it up at the Mother and Baby group.'

'Should I give the doctor a ring?'

'No need for that at the moment. I know what to watch out for, and the rash hasn't broken out yet so we don't know if it really is chickenpox. Of course this puts paid to our trip to Devon. Quite apart from seeing Jerry I was looking forward to a few days away, especially after all that's been going on here.'

'I wish I could stay here and give you a hand, love, but I'm afraid I'll have to go on without you. It is my job, after all. Is there anything I can do for you before I leave?'

'You can go and get Vera Hatch to open up the shop, and see if she has any calamine lotion. I'll need it when the blisters come out. And see if she has a small roll of cotton wool, or better still, wadding. I'll have to make him a pair of little mittens to stop him scratching.'

'Right-ho. Anything else?'

'I could kill for a box of Rowntree's Black Magic! If I have to sit up for umpteen nights on end with an unhappy baby I'm going to need energy.'

* * *

As Dick told Maudie on his return home some days later, he was allowed into a small ward on the second floor of the big hospital. 'I refuse to say that I was *admitted*,' he said, half sheepishly, 'because that sounds as if I was joining the patients as one of their number!'

'Rather grim, was it?'

'Actually it wasn't as bad as I expected. I didn't see any padded cells, although undoubtedly they have some of them hidden away somewhere on the premises. Jerry's ward has six beds, and I found him sitting in an armchair, gazing out of the window at some rather pleasant grounds.'

'Did he speak to you? Did he remember who you are?'

'He did seem to, after a bit of prompting. I stretched the truth a bit and said you remembered the nice afternoon you had together when he came to tea, and that you wondered if he might have noticed where you'd put the tie belt from your spotted dress, because you couldn't find it. He started to weep then and told me he'd taken it while you were out of the room. He knew he shouldn't have done it but he only wanted a little something to remember you by.

'According to him he stuffed it in his pocket on the spur of the moment. After leaving here he lost his way and ended up in the glebe by accident. Then he had to retrace his steps to the fork in the lane to get to the Spread Eagle. When he got to his room he went to put the belt away in his samples case, and that's when he found it missing from his pocket. It must have fallen out when he pulled out his handkerchief to blow his nose. He admitted he was feeling so weak and depressed after that that he lay down on his bed and cried like a baby. It doesn't seem to take much to set him off.

'That's when he started to sing, Maudie. It was really weird. He almost seemed to be far away somewhere, He must have remembered that game kids used to play in the schoolyard when we were young:

I sent a letter to my love
And on the way I lost it
One of you has picked it up
And put it in your pocket.

'After that he was well gone and I couldn't get through to him any more. It was no good. I had to come away.'

Maudie burst into tears. Dick reached

over and took her hand in his. 'Come on, love, it isn't that bad.'

'Oh, don't mind me,' she said, sniffing. 'I've had rather an exhausting week with young Charlie and it's made me feel a bit weepy, that's all. Do you think if I sent Jerry another remembrance of me they'd let him keep it? A snap of you and me together, perhaps, or a lace-edged handkerchief? Something small he could keep in the pocket of his dressing gown, or his bedside locker?'

'It wouldn't hurt to try,' Dick said, thinking that the action would be more of a comfort to Maudie than to Jerry Saunders, who was fast losing his grip on reality.

Dick went to write up his report and Maudie went upstairs to check on their son, who was now covered in a mixture of bumps, fluid-filled blisters, and healing scabs. 'Drink!' he croaked, lifting his little arms to be picked up.

She sat beside him with the sides of the cot down, coaxing him to take more of the Lucozade she'd brought upstairs with her. Pleased when he gulped down a cupful, she poured some more out of the bottle, hoping that this signalled a return of his appetite, which had been almost non-existent since Dick had left for Devon. She gave a sigh of relief. Just a few more days to go, and then, all being well, Charlie would be returned to health, and perhaps her own personal nightmare would be over. With any luck she would be exonerated in the eyes of Llandyfan when the true story of the disappearing belt got out. She said as much to Dick when he looked in to kiss his son goodnight.

'That's if we can persuade the newspapers to run the story,' she muttered. 'It seems they're always quick to write a lot of nonsense but do they put matters right when the truth cones out? No, of course they don't. The most you ever get is a small paragraph buried on page sixteen saying they were misinformed, and sorry for the inconvenience. Pah!'

'Never mind the papers. What we need to do is tell it to some local who would be sure to pass it around to all the world. Should we ask the vicar to proclaim it from the pulpit?' He smiled. 'No, that won't do. Not everybody goes to church. Do we know any women who can't keep their tongues from clacking?'

Maudie and Dick looked at each other. 'Vera Hatch!' they said in unison.

'Atch!' Charlie shouted.

'Somebody is on the mend!' Dick said, delighted.

*   *   *

'The poor man!' Joan Blunt said, rubbing the back of her hand across her eyes. 'One can only hope that he'll be put right in the end, although it doesn't sound very hopeful.'

The two friends were sitting in the vicarage garden, enjoying the last warm days of autumn. Charlie, now fully recovered, was sitting on a blanket on the grass, lifting his little hands to try to catch a butterfly. Perkin, lurking nearby, leapt up to catch the pretty thing, missing by inches. The toddler clapped his hands and screamed his approval. The two ladies clapped their hands over their ears.

'There's nothing wrong with his lungs, is there?' Mrs Blunt observed. 'But about this sad business of Verity Bourne, Nurse. Does this mean that you've been completely exonerated now? I do hope so.'

Maudie bit her lip. 'DI Goodman told Dick that I'm in the clear as far as he can see and that I shan't be prosecuted.'

'As far as he can see! What is that supposed to mean?'

'It means there's no evidence to say I was anywhere near the glebe when Miss Bourne was killed, but unfortunately I don't have any alibi, either.'

'But Mr Saunders' testimony? Surely that explains how your belt found its way from your home to the glebe?'

'It does if it's true. The trouble is that he first made a false confession of having killed Verity himself. He'd got the idea from that awful newspaper article that I was being accused and thought he could save me. Now of course he's obviously mentally unsound, so what does all that add up to? His story about the belt could be just another falsehood, or the product of his disturbed mind.'

'Then we'll just hope and pray that the real killer is found,' Mrs Blunt said, reaching down to wave off a fly that had settled on the top of Charlie's sun hat.

26

Dick had gone back to work, and Maudie had decided to give the cottage a good going over. Having been so busy with Charlie during his illness she'd had to let the housework go and there was a disgraceful layer of dust all over the polished surfaces of the sitting room furniture.

She had just settled Charlie in his playpen with a stack of colourful nesting tumblers to hold his attention, when the doorbell rang. There was no answering bark from Rover, who must have wandered off on business of his own. If that was another newspaper reporter . . . She ran to the kitchen and picked up a wet floor mop. If Rover couldn't be relied upon to see him off, then she jolly well would!

She opened the door to a dishevelled-looking woman with the beginnings of a fine black eye. The visitor stepped back in alarm at the sight of this irate figure brandishing the dripping mop, and Maudie hastened to reassure her.

'I'm so sorry. I was just — er — can I help you?'

'Are you the midwife?'

'Yes, I am, but I'm afraid I'm not seeing patients just now. I can give you the number to call, though, or you can always dial 999 if it's urgent.'

'But ain't you the one whose hubby is a copper, like?'

'You'd better come in and tell me what this is all about.' Maudie stood aside to let the woman come in. Whatever this was all about it beat vacuuming and dusting, hands down!

'Now then, Mrs . . . '

'Lunney. Edith Polley as was.'

Eddie Lunney's mother! With a great effort Maudie managed to keep an expression of distaste from crossing her face. It was all down to this woman's child, and his grandmother, that her involvement with Verity Bourne had begun, and see how that had ended! *Count to ten, Maudie!*

'How can I help you, Mrs Lunney?'

'It's him, Nurse, My Nate. He's locked me out, and I don't know what to do. I could go up my mum's but I know what she'd say. She's always on at me to leave him, but whenever I say I might do that she says I'm a married woman and that means I've made my bed and now I must lie in it.'

'How would you like a cup of tea, Mrs Lunney? Then we'll have a nice chat and you can tell me all about it.'

'I don't mind if I do. I didn't have no breakfast this morning.'

Maudie made a brew and put a few Marie biscuits on a plate. She would listen to what the woman had to say; having someone to confide in would do the poor thing good. But she wasn't a social worker, and she knew better than to get in the middle of a dispute between husband and wife, unless it had something to do with the pregnancy of the mother. She had no wish to sport a black eye to match Mrs Lunney's.

'Now then: would you like to tell me what's worrying you?'

'Like I said, Nurse, he's locked me out. I took our Eddie to school like always, and when I got back the door was shut fast. I shouted and banged, and I know he was in there, but he never come to open it.'

'Are you sure he was at home?'

'Where else would he be at that time of day before the pubs open?'

Where, indeed? Maudie guessed that the man hadn't gone to an early-morning weekday church service; that was certain.

'Has this ever happened before, Mrs Lunney?'

'Sometimes, when he's been drinking. One time I had to stay the night in the outdoor privy before he come to his senses; raining it was, too, and the roof leaks.'

'What about your poor eye, Mrs Lunney? And please don't tell me you walked into a lamppost. I've heard that one before.'

'It was all on account of last night's supper. Kicked up a fuss because it was macaroni cheese. I tells him if he wants meat he'd better fork over the means to pay for it instead of lining Len Frost's pockets down the Spread Eagle. Besides, macaroni cheese is our Eddie's favourite. And I should have held my tongue for that's when Nate let me have it. I'll teach you to answer back, he says, and the boy looking on, taking it all in.'

No wonder little Eddie was becoming a bully, with that sort of example. 'Has he always been like this, Mrs Lunney?'

'I s'pose so, but he's been a lot worse lately. It's lucky he's away for months at a time. If I had him under my feet every day I don't know what I'd do, and that's a fact.'

'He's in the merchant navy, isn't he?'

'Yes, that's right. Sails all over the world, he does. Makes good money when he remembers to send it home, and he's good to the boy. Always bringing him some little gadget or toy from foreign parts. Not this last time, though. It's my belief something bad happened to him on this trip. Maybe he got a bad report from the captain because he's had no word of another ship yet. He should be thinking of signing on again by now, instead of sitting at home, drinking himself silly.'

'So what is it you'd like me to do, Mrs Lunney?'

'Oh, not you, Nurse! It's your hubby I was hoping to see. I thought if he had a word with Nate, warned him to keep his fists to himself, it might make him stop and think.'

'I'm sorry, Mrs Lunney, but Dick doesn't deal with that sort of thing any more. You need to contact Midvale and they'll send a constable to speak to you.'

'But isn't your hubby the village constable? That's what it says in the paper!'

Maudie sighed. That beastly newspaper again! 'Dick is a Detective Sergeant now. I'm afraid he doesn't deal with domestic problems unless something like murder is involved.'

'Then I come to the wrong place. I'd best not hold you up, then, or when your hubby gets home and finds no dinner on the table, you'll be the one with a black eye, same as me.'

Sadly, Maudie watched the woman go, marching down the street like a prisoner on his way to execution. Never in a million years would Dick strike his wife, or even grumble if his meal was delayed, not that he was due home for lunch in any case. It was a sad reflection on the state of marriage that Edith Lunney would consider it to be a possibility.

★ ★ ★

When Dick arrived home that evening he was delighted to find his favourite meal awaiting him. Corned beef, creamy mashed potatoes, and an assortment of the vegetables grown in his own garden. 'And jam roly poly with lashings of custard to follow, unless you'd prefer golden syrup with it,' Maudie told him.

'Well! This is just what the doctor ordered, old girl!' he told her, beaming. 'To what do I owe the pleasure of a slap-up meal like this in the middle of the week?'

'Nothing is too good for my darling husband,' she told him, kissing him on his bald patch as he sat down at the table.

'You're not hoping to get round me for something, are you? This tea isn't your way of softening me up?'

'Never in this world. I've just been counting my blessings, and it so happens you are one of them!'

He cast her a look of deep suspicion. 'Just what have you been up to today, Maudie Bryant? is there something I should know?'

'I had a visit from that Edith Lunney today, Dick.'

'Young Eddie's mother.'

'That's right. Actually she came to see you.'

'I always knew I was irresistible to women.'

'Fool! You know her husband is home from sea. Well, it seems he's been throwing his weight around, in more ways than one. He gave her a black eye last night and this morning he's locked her out of the house. Like everyone else she's been reading the *Pilot* and she came here because she thinks you're the village bobby.'

Dick shrugged. 'It wouldn't have done her any good if I was. I've seen this sort of thing before, and so have you. Nothing can be done unless she agrees to press charges, and when it comes to the crunch she won't do it. If he gets put inside he won't be able to earn a living, and she and the boy will suffer for it. And she knows what she'll get when he comes out of prison, wanting to get even with her.'

'So she'll consider her options and decide to make the best of a bad job,' Maudie said. 'Eat up, Dick, and I'll go and dish up your jam roll.'

27

A tearful small boy stood on the doorstep. 'Can I help you?' Maudie asked, with a reassuring smile.

'Please, miss, I want to see the policeman,' the child said, rubbing his eyes with dirty fists.

'You've come to the wrong place, dear. My husband is a Detective Sergeant. Perhaps you need Constable Salter; he's the village policeman now. You'll find him in the little white house near the Spread Eagle.'

'No miss. I want a detective.'

'I see. And what seems to be the problem?'

'My Gran's dog's gone missing. Detectives find clues, don't they?'

'Indeed they do, but dogs often go for a little walk on their own, you know. Perhaps he'll come home on his own after a while.'

'It's not a he, it's a her. And she's all

upset cos my grandad died and she's all alone except for her.'

It took Maudie a minute or two to straighten out this tangle. 'Just wait there while I fetch a pencil and paper,' she told him. 'You can give me the details and I'll let my husband know when he gets home.'

'All right, miss, but you won't forget, will you?'

'I won't forget, and I promise I'll keep a good look out for your gran's dog, when I'm out walking my own. What's her name?'

'Mrs Peever.'

'I meant the dog.'

'Flossie. What's your dog called? Can I see him?'

But Rover, when called, was nowhere to be found.

⋆ ⋆ ⋆

Maudie had no sooner arranged herself on the settee, ready for a well-deserved nap, when the doorbell rang again. Muttering, she got up and flung the door open.

'I'm sorry, but my husband isn't at

home,' she began, breaking off in mid-flow when she recognized the apologetic figure of the infants' teacher, clutching an overstuffed handbag.

'Mrs Snead! How lovely to see you! Do come in.'

'I hope I'm not disturbing you,' that lady began, eyeing the crocheted blanket that had slid to the floor when Maudie got up.

'Not at all. Do sit down.'

'Thank you. Actually it was your husband I was hoping to see.'

You and the rest of the village, Maudie thought, but didn't say. Why couldn't people telephone Midvale, or at least dial 999 if there was an emergency? Why disturb the poor chap at home? 'Can I give my husband a message, Mrs Snead?'

'Actually, now I'm here, I feel a bit silly. Perhaps I shouldn't have come. It's just that I felt a bit worried when it first happened. Of course I had to wait until school was dismissed for the day, and now I'm not quite as upset as I was earlier.'

Maudie put on her most sympathetic

expression. 'Would you like to confide in me, Mrs Snead? You know what they say about a trouble shared.'

'It was halfway through the morning. Eddie Lunney's father appeared in the doorway of my classroom, quite obviously drunk. Fortunately the children had gone out to play or they would have been frightened, I know. I felt a bit scared myself, for Miss Rice was outside on playground duty and she wouldn't have heard me if I'd had to call for help. The children make such a noise when they are dashing about in the playground.'

'And what did the man have to say for himself?'

'A lot of nonsense about how he'd come to take his son home. To quote him exactly, 'I don't want no woman teacher for my boy. How's that supposed to make a man of him?' I told him to go and see the vicar about it and that until the school board manages to hire a male teacher, Eddie will just have to put up with me!'

'That was brave of you. Nate Lunney is known to be free with his fists.'

Mrs Snead grinned. 'I happened to

have the cane handy and I grabbed it up and advanced on him, shaking it as if I meant to give him six of the best! The brute turned tail and ran. That's the way to deal with bullies, Mrs Bryant! Give them no quarter, I say, and they'll soon think better of threatening defenseless victims.'

'Let's hope he remembers that if he goes to see Mr Blunt,' Maudie said. She didn't like to think of the elderly vicar suffering violence at the hands of the brutal sailor. A man who could black his wife's eye would probably have no respect for a man of the cloth, either.

'Perhaps if you mention this to your husband he might send someone to speak to Lunney,' Mrs Snead said. 'Warn him off or something. Do you know, Mrs Bryant, when the fellow was standing there, ranting and raving, something sort of clicked in my mind, a sort of déjà vu. I could have sworn I'd seen him somewhere before but of course I couldn't have. I'm told he's been away at sea for months and, as you know, I've only recently arrived here.'

'Before you go, do you know a Mrs Peever? I believe she lives up at the prefabs.'

'Well yes, as a matter of fact I do. An elderly widow, like myself. Why do you ask? She hasn't had trouble with Lunney, has she?'

'Not as far as I know. Her grandson was here earlier, asking to see my husband. Apparently her little dog has gone missing and the little boy thought that a police detective could find her.'

'A dear little poodle, I believe. I'll keep a good lookout for it on my way home. Such a shame if anything has happened to it. The poor soul dotes on it, I understand.'

Closing the door behind her visitor, Maudie wondered what she should do in the event of Nate Lunney turning up here. She really must keep the doors firmly locked in future, and get into the habit of looking though the peephole before she opened up.

Happy cries came from above her head, and she started upstairs to see to Charlie. No chance of a nap for her now, she realized. Rover still seemed to be missing, which was odd, and she felt slightly uneasy because he seldom strayed far from the cottage. He was too fond of his home comforts for that. And now there were two dogs missing. It was too soon to start worrying about hit-and-run car drivers or dognappers yet it wouldn't hurt to go out for a little while to have a look around. Rover had probably found something horrid to roll in and he was unlikely to come home until his coat was a thorough mess.

'Come on, Charlie! Let's get you changed and we'll take you for a little ride.'

'Ikle?' he asked, brightening up.

'No, not your fairy cycle this time. We'll take the pushchair. We've got to go and look for Rover.'

'Ikle!' he roared. 'Want ikle!'

* * *

Maudie set out, pushing a tear-stained Charlie in his buggy. Deprived of her nap, she felt like having a tantrum herself. All in all it had been quite a day, and now she was faced with the prospect of hauling the pushchair over the rough ground of the glebe. She almost turned back, but the lane on the other side of the glebe led to the prefabs, and if Flossie had wandered off, it made sense that she might have come this way.

Then she caught sight of them. Two small dogs, yelping and happily dashing about, side by side. One was Rover, her faithful forty-nine-varieties mongrel and the other was an absolutely filthy pedigree poodle, who might possibly be white underneath all that grime.

'Rover! Here, boy!'

Rover came racing up, barking happily. His new found friend wasn't far behind and she, too, greeted Maudie joyously. 'Down, girl! Down, I say! Just look at the condition you're in! Just wait until your mistress sees you! Get off home now. Shoo! Shoo!'

But Flossie refused to be dismissed and in the end Maudie returned home, with the two dogs racing ahead of the pushchair. Charlie, thrilled by it all, shouted and clapped all the way back.

What a sight they must present to the world, Maudie thought. Two absolutely filthy dogs, a woman with torn stockings and a muddy skirt, and a noisy toddler, exercising his lungs to the utmost. Luckily the village street was deserted when they reached the cottage. She let Flossie into the scullery and filled Rover's bowl with fresh water, which the poodle lapped at thirstily. Dick could run the little dog back to Mrs Peever after tea.

Meanwhile she hoped that nobody had seen her bringing Flossie inside. Her own reputation was bad enough these days without someone spreading the word that she was going about snatching other people's pets.

28

Unfortunately Dick called to say he'd been held up at work. 'We've had rather a busy day here, looking into what was reported to us as a possible murder. Some boys, playing about where they shouldn't have been, found a body in an abandoned house on the other side of Brookfield. In the end it turned out to be a death due to natural causes, or so we think; an old tramp, well known to the police, who probably just broke in there to curl up and die.'

'Sad, though.'

'True, but there were no signs of violence on the body, so unless the post-mortem shows up something untoward, that will be the end of it as far as we're concerned. The chief is holding a press conference and I have to be there to back him up. After that I have paperwork to catch up on. If I let it slide I'll never catch up. Everything all right with you and the boy?'

'Oh, yes. Busy day. I have a few interesting things to tell you, but they can keep until you get here.'

'Right-ho! See you around nine, then, if I'm lucky.'

Maudie went back to the kitchen, just in time to rescue the sausages she'd left sitting out on the table when the phone rang. They wouldn't be needed now but they'd do for tomorrow if kept safely on the marble slab in the larder. She could make do with a poached egg for her own tea, and if Dick was hungry when he came home, he could have the same thing, with toast.

The two dogs watched her, tails wagging. 'What am I to do with you, Flossie?' she demanded. 'I don't suppose you'd find your way home if I put you outside? No, of course you wouldn't. You'd rather stay out on the lam. Better to keep you here until we can take you home, and after that it's down to your mistress to keep you out of trouble.'

Maudie fervently hoped that Flossie wasn't in heat. It would be most unfortunate if this encounter resulted in the arrival of half a dozen or more miniature Rovers. What would you call puppies who were a mixture of mongrel and poodle? Mongoodles? Poogrels? Either way Flossie's owner would be less than delighted.

Maudie returned to the telephone. If they couldn't return Flossie to Mrs Peever tonight, she could at least put the woman's mind at ease. Unfortunately the lady didn't seem to be on the phone for there was no Peever listed in the directory.

* * *

The following day being Saturday, Dick was at home all day, so after breakfast they started out for the prefabs, with his car bursting at the seams. Maudie sat in the passenger seat with Charlie on her lap and the two dogs lay on the back seat, looking out of the windows with interest. Maudie had become quite fond of the little poodle overnight and would be sorry to hand her back.

'You take her in,' Dick said. 'You're the one who found the animal; you may as well get the grateful thanks. I'll wait out here with Charlie and Rover.'

Mrs Peever was overjoyed to welcome her errant pet home. 'And to think you were in that nasty glebe, my darling!' she scolded. She shook her head at Maudie. 'That was where my former lodger was found dead, and my poor darling Flossie might have gone the same way!'

Maudie's ears pricked up. 'Your former lodger?'

'Oh, yes, poor Miss Bourne. She stayed with me for a day or two when she first came to the school, but it didn't last. I was lonely after my hubby died and finding it hard to make ends meet, so I thought I'd try taking in paying guests. Mrs Beasley — do you know Cora Beasley? — sent Miss Bourne to me, but I'm afraid it failed from the word go. Not to speak ill of the dead, but she was a difficult person — most difficult, in fact — and when she complained about my poor Flossie leaving white hairs on her skirts why, she had to go. Anyone who can complain about an innocent dog is no fit company in my book.'

Not much chance of anyone getting

covered in white hairs at the moment, Maudie thought, looking at the poodle's filthy coat. 'So she left?'

'She found lodgings with a widow woman on the next street.'

'And did you ever see her again?'

'Not exactly, although a man did come here asking for her. I gave him directions to her new place, and that was that.'

'What sort of man? Can you recall what he looked like? Was it one of the school governors, perhaps, or a parent of one of her pupils?'

'I'd never seen him before, but I'm sure I'd recognize him again, Big. Burly. Fists like hams. And he walked with a sort of roll, if you know what I mean.'

'Did he frighten you, Mrs Peever?'

'Oh no, dear. He was quite polite, I thought, although a bit of a rough diamond. He didn't threaten me in any way, although I did wonder what business the poor girl had with a great hulk like that.'

Definitely not one of the school governors, then. 'Mrs Peever, would you mind if I bring my husband in to hear this? He's a Detective Sergeant and I know he'd find it interesting.'

'I don't know what I have said that would interest your husband, Mrs Bryant, but do bring him in, by all means.'

So while Dick went inside to hear Mrs Peever's story Maudie waited with Charlie, in a state of high excitement. When he emerged a few minutes later she couldn't wait to hear what had transpired, but Dick only shrugged.

'Get in the car, old girl and let's get home. I have some tidying up that needs doing in the garden, and I'd like to get on with it before it starts to rain.'

Fuming, she did as she was told, but when they were on the road she nudged him with her elbow. 'Come on, Dick. Spill the beans!'

'I don't know what you want me to say. The lady simply repeated what she had said to you; word for word, I'd say. The girl had a gentleman caller; Mrs Peever explained that she no longer lived there, and gave him directions to her new place of residence.'

'But don't you think it means something?'

'So what if a man did call on Verity Bourne? It's a free country. It could have been anybody, Maudie: a brother, a cousin, an old boy friend.'

Maudie played her trump card. 'I suppose so, but it sounds like Nate Lunney to me. The point is, what could he want with Verity Bourne?'

'Isn't it obvious? She'd caned his little boy and Lunney wanted to have it out with her.'

'I still think he did it.'

Cursing, Dick swerved to avoid a cat that had appeared out of nowhere and had darted across the road in front of the car. Rover hurled himself about in the back seat, barking, and, frightened by the commotion, Charlie began to wail. Seeing her husband's clenched jaw, Maudie felt it wise to let the matter drop. That didn't stop her thinking, however.

The dates didn't add up. Verity Bourne hadn't died at that point. She'd gone on to become a thorn in Maudie's side, and whichever way you looked at it Nate Lunney — if it was he who had been Mrs Peever's visitor — had not killed the school teacher, or at least, not then.

But Verity Bourne was dead, and somebody was responsible. If not Lunney, then who? What they needed was one of those identification parades you saw in Hollywood movies. Several men, all bearing a slight resemblance to each other, standing in line, holding up numbered cards in front of them. Mrs Peever, trembling with anxiety, peering at each of them intently, before whispering the number of the man she recognized to the officer in charge. Nate Lunney!

But Maudie knew her husband well enough to gauge his response if she suggested such a thing. There were no grounds for bringing in Nate Lunney on suspicion of murder. No proof that he had eventually caught up with Verity, or been anywhere near the glebe on the day of her death. We did not live in a police state and British bobbies did not swoop down on all and sundry, accusing them of crimes they hadn't committed. And his boss, DI Goodman, would certainly say that the police knew what they were doing, thank you very much, and they needed no help from amateur detectives.

Maudie had to admit that they would probably be right. And even if they did collar the man and take him in for questioning they'd probably have to release him again for lack of evidence, and what might happen then? His poor wife would probably come in for a beating, and when he discovered who had been responsible for his humiliation, Mrs Peever would be made to suffer for it, too.

29

Maudie confided in her friend, Joan Blunt, who looked sceptical.

'Do you really think he did it, Nurse? This Nate Lunney?'

'I don't know, but somebody certainly did, and I do wish they'd catch the chap who's responsible, and deal with him accordingly. How is anyone supposed to feel safe in the meantime? It's bad enough if the killer had a motive for doing away with the poor woman, but if it was just a random act by some lunatic he's likely to strike again, at any time!'

'After what you've told me about the way Lunney has been treating his poor wife I wondered if I ought to go and see her. I'm sure she could use some moral support. The only thing is, when I mentioned it to Harold he said it probably wouldn't be a good idea. The Lunneys aren't Church of England and it might be looked on as interference and that could set the man off again.'

'My thoughts exactly.'

'So that's why I think that you should be the one to call round, Nurse.'

'Me!'

'Why not? She did confide in you, after all, and you'd be doing her a kindness by looking in to see how she is. I do think she'd be grateful to know that somebody understands her situation and cares about her, even though she can't be persuaded to report him to the authorities.'

Maudie shook her head. 'Dick won't like it if I do. And to tell you the truth I'm none too keen to get myself in any deeper after what I've been through recently.'

'It was just a thought, Nurse. My husband is probably right, and we should mind our own business, although I must admit it makes me think of the story of the Good Samaritan. A neighbour is in trouble and I'm among those who have chosen to pass by on the other side.'

Perkin strolled into the room then and hopped up on her lap, purring loudly. The conversation turned to household pets and Maudie described her encounter with the poodle, Flossie, and her fears that she might have been made responsible for a litter of puppies. 'It's all right, though, I'm glad so say. Mrs Peever assured me that the animal has been spayed. She couldn't be doing with all that worry at her time of life, that's what she said. I'm a good thirty years younger, and I can't be doing with it, either. I've enough on my plate bringing human babies into the world, although I'm afraid that's all behind me now.'

'You miss it, don't you, Nurse? Being a midwife, I mean?'

'I'm busy enough at present with a child of my own to look after, and a husband as well, but I do feel sad to think I may never deliver another baby. That moment when you place a healthy baby in its mother's arms, and see the love on her face, and you can say that both of them have come safely through their ordeal and that you, the nurse, have helped with that, it's the best feeling in the world, Mrs Blunt!'

'I'm sure it is,' her friend said, smiling.

★ ★ ★

That afternoon Maudie set out for a stroll, with Charlie in his pushchair and Rover striding out in front, pausing every now and then to investigate some enticing smell along the way. It was, she assured herself, simply coincidence that their route led them past the Lunneys' tumbledown cottage, but having arrived at the garden gate it seemed a pity to pass by without stopping to have a word with Edith Lunney.

Maudie wondered who their landlord was. The place could certainly do with some sprucing up. There were slates missing from the roof, and it must have been years since the doors and window ledges had seen a fresh coat of paint. Someone had made an effort to grow a few vegetables in a nearby plot, but all that remained now were a few spindly cabbages, nothing like the robust specimens grown by Dick.

She rapped at the back door, and after a moment the frightened face of Edith Lunney appeared at the kitchen window. 'I was passing by and I thought I'd just pop in to see how you are,' Maudie began, when the door was opened at last.

'Do you want to come in? I'm sure the little boy will be all right sitting in his chair in the fresh air.'

Maudie stepped inside. The kitchen was neat enough, and there were fresh white curtains hanging at the window, and a geranium in a pot on the windowsill.

'I'm afraid I can't offer you a cup of tea or anything,' the woman said, her gaze dropping to a pail beside the kitchen sink. 'My hubby had a drop too many in the Spread Eagle last night and when he came home he got a bit awkward.'

Awkward indeed, Maudie thought, looking at the remains of what looked like a whole tea service in the bucket.

'If you'd like me to have a word with my husband . . . ' she began.

'Not much he can do, unless he's got a magic pill to make Nate stop drinking. If he could just get a ship and get back to sea we'd be all right here, Eddie and me. It's not having nowhere to go that gets him down, see. But he seems to have been in some sort of trouble during his last voyage and word gets around, don't it?

The ships' masters don't want no troublemakers on board, not during a long voyage like Nate's used to.'

'Have you any idea what that trouble may have been?' Maudie asked, but her words were interrupted by the roar of a man who had been disturbed from sleep. Horrified, she looked towards the source of the noise and saw the bulk of Nate Lunney, filling the doorway of what was obviously the entrance to an inner room.

'Who's this, then?' he bellowed, advancing into the kitchen. 'I thought I told you not to let no nosy parkers into my house, you stupid good-for-nothing woman. Mebbe you want another dose of what you got last night, eh?'

'That will be quite enough of that!' Maudie rapped out. Although she was desperately frightened inside she had precipitated this by being foolish enough the come here and she couldn't allow his wife to suffer for it.

'Oh, yeah? And who do you think you are, missus, telling a man what he can do in his own house? Who are you, hey? Come from the Social, have you, sticking your nose in where it's not wanted?'

'If you must know, I'm a policeman's wife,' Maudie said, hoping to intimidate him. It didn't work.

'We'll see about that!' he roared, bounding towards her. She braced herself for the blow that didn't come. Holding her elbow in a painful grip he pushed her out through the kitchen door, past Charlie in his pushchair, past the empty clothesline, towards a sagging privy that was half hidden by leafless lilac bushes. Opening the door with his free hand he thrust her inside, slamming the door shut after her. Gasping for breath she heard what sounded like a bar being rammed home in its sockets.

Holding her nose against the stench she looked around her, straining her eyes against the gloom. There was nothing she could use as a weapon, nothing that might be employed to break the door down. The facility, if you could call it that, was nothing but a plank with two round holes carved in it. She leaned against the wall, wondering what too next. She was certainly not going to sit down on that, although if she didn't get out of here soon it she might have to make use of it.

In the distance, Charlie began to wail. She waited. His cries grew louder. She began to pound on the rough wooden door, getting a splinter in her hand in the process. She sucked her finger. 'Let me out! Let me out, I say! Will you open this door!'

Hearing her cries Rover came and scrabbled at the door, barking wildly, which did nothing to help the situation. In the end he was making so much noise that at first she didn't hear the barrier being removed. Then she realized she was about to be released and she tensed, fearing what Nate Lunney must be planning to do next. Was she going to be beaten? Strangled, even? How could she defend herself against such a great brute of a man? If only she had something to use as a weapon! But her handbag was attached to the handle of the pushchair and she didn't have so much as a hairpin upon her person. Muttering a hasty prayer for deliverance, she prepared to meet her fate.

30

The door flew open to reveal Mrs Lunney, accompanied by Charlie in his pushchair, and Rover, who was frisking around as if they were just enjoying a happy day out.

'Come on, madam, do. We've got to get out of here before he comes round. He'll be that mad when he does, I wouldn't give a penny for either of our lives if he catches up with us.'

'What's happened?' Maudie wanted to know, snatching the handle of Charlie's chair from the other woman's grasp.

'I laid him out with the frying pan. He was just taking off his belt to give me a thrashing so I grabbed the pan and let him have it. It wasn't washed, neither. He'll have bits of bacon fat all over his head when he comes to.'

'Good!' said Maudie. 'He'll have more than that to worry about when my Dick gets hold of him.'

'Do come *on*, madam! You don't know him like I do! He'll kill us, I know he will!'

The two women scuttled off, looking back as they went. When they reached the main road Maudie attempted to flag down an approaching car which, thankfully, slowed down a few yards from them. In all her days at Llandyfan she had never been so glad to see the Reverend Harold Blunt as she was at that moment.

'Is anything wrong, Nurse?'

'Oh, thank goodness! Can you give us a lift home, please, vicar? Mrs Lunney's husband is on the rampage and we're afraid for our lives!'

The vicar raised his eyebrows in smiling disbelief but nevertheless he did as she asked. 'Anything to help a lady in distress,' he said, as he bundled the pushchair into the boot and helped the women into the vicarage car. 'Your dog seems to have disappeared, Nurse,' he said, handing Charlie to his mother. 'Will he be all right?'

'Yes, yes. I'm sure he can find his own way home,' Maudie mumbled, almost holding her breath. 'Please, can we just get going? I really have to contact Dick as soon as possible.'

★　★　★

Much later, Maudie described the scene to Dick who, mercifully, refrained from scolding her for her folly in what she had done. 'I thought I was done for when the door opened, but it was Mrs Lunney who stood there instead of him. We simply pelted down the lane, and if you'd ever tried that wearing a skirt and high-heeled shoes you'd know how difficult that is!'

'Those shoes could have come in handy, though,' Dick said. 'Another time you should just hold one by the toe, and gouge the chap in the eye with the heel. Just the ticket to make him back off, especially with those metal reinforcements you've had put on to save them wearing down.'

Maudie shuddered, distressed at the thought of ever coming near enough to the murderous Lunney to be able to stab him in the eye. 'There won't be a next time!'

'Not as far as he's concerned, anyway. We've got him safely tucked up in a cell, and there he's going to stay.'

'But what if Edith won't press charges? She is his wife, after all.'

'That no longer matters. Nate Lunney has questions to answer. Mrs Snead has now come forward with some very useful information.'

'Mrs Snead? She's a newcomer to the village. What can she possibly know about anything?'

'Ah, now, we'll just have to wait and see, won't we?'

This annoyed Maudie very much, for she longed to know what the infants' teacher had to say to the police, and she doubted very much if Dick would be able to satisfy her curiosity while the case was ongoing.

But later that day the lady herself arrived at the door, just back from a trip to police headquarters at Midvale and eager to share her news.

'Poor Mrs Lunney was waiting with me at the police station when I went there to give evidence, and she told me what that beastly man put you through the other day,' she said, when Maudie had all but dragged her inside, and was about to ply her with tea and biscuits.

'I know I gave you a hint the other day that I had something at the back of my mind, and I thought you'd like to hear the sequel. That Detective Inspector did say something about my keeping quiet until the case comes to trial, but you don't count, do you? Your hubby is a detective and I'm sure he shares all the details of his cases with you.'

'Oh, yes,' Maudie fibbed. She had to hear what was coming next, and Dick need never know. 'You've remembered something, you said?'

'Well, it was when Lunney came to the school the other day, shouting the odds about female teachers. It called to mind something I'd seen before.'

'Go on.'

'It was about a year ago, at my last school, in Liverpool. After I retired they used to get me to go back occasionally, to take on little projects with the children. I had them making a model of a medieval village at the time, I remember, and they were just so interested, it was really quite rewarding for me.'

'And that was it? A model village? I don't quite see . . . '

'Sorry. I'm getting carried away. Well, I was in the school office when a man burst in there, demanding to see one of the teachers. The school secretary explained that the teacher in question was busy with her class and couldn't be disturbed, and if it was a matter of a problem with his child, would he like to speak to the headmaster? He stamped out then, but later, when I was leaving to go home, I noticed him hanging around the school gates. The thing is, Mrs Bryant, I'm absolutely sure now that the man was Nate Lunney. The two episodes hang together in my mind.'

Maudie sat forward eagerly. 'And what about the teacher he demanded to see, the one in Liverpool? I know that Miss Bourne came from there. Could she have been the one he wanted to see?'

Mrs Snead shook her head. 'I really have no idea. As I said, she wasn't summoned because she was teaching her class. And it wouldn't have proved a thing if I'd got a look at her because I never met Miss Bourne after I came here. Ships that pass in the night, you see.'

It was all starting to fall into place for Maudie now. 'Nate Lunney and Verity Bourne knew each other in Liverpool. He goes back to sea and she moves to Llandyfan to teach. He comes back to England when his tour of duty is up and of course he returns to his family here. He finds out that Verity is here now, so he goes to Mrs Peever's house to speak to her. She, in turn, sends him on to Miss Bourne's new lodgings. And then . . . '

'And then he killed her!' Mrs Snead cried, twisting her hand in a graphic display of manual strangulation that made Maudie shiver. 'But why? What had she done?'

'If you're right about them having known each other in Liverpool, the murder can't have had anything to do with Miss Bourne giving little Eddie the cane,' Maudie said. 'She must have done something else that he wanted to pay her back for. Perhaps she cheated him out of money, or reported him to the police for some crime she'd witnessed.'

'Or she was trying to blackmail him over what she'd seen,' Mrs Snead said, bright-eyed with excitement. 'Teachers are notoriously poorly paid, you know.'

Maudie laughed. 'Don't you think we're getting rather carried away? We can speculate all we like, but I don't suppose we'll ever get to the bottom of all this.'

But she was wrong. The answer, when it came, was a simple one, and the motive for the killing was as old as time itself.

★　★　★

Dick did not come home that night. Having received a message not to expect him Maudie decided to turn in early and try to lose herself in her new library book. Before she went upstairs she locked and bolted all the doors and then, having done so, she went back downstairs and tested them again. Nate Lunney was safely locked up, yet nothing had yet been proved against him and the real murderer could be lurking nearby. At one point Rover gave a low growl and she shot up in bed, straining her ears to try to identify the cause of his alarm, but she could hear nothing untoward and the dog did not stir again.

At two o'clock she was still awake and she got out of bed, determined to go down and make herself a cup of tea. Or perhaps cocoa would be best at this time of night since Charlie would have her up early in the morning? For once she would be glad to hear him bellowing at five a.m. as he sometimes did. It would be good to greet the daylight. The dark hours led to too many fears and sobering thoughts.

* * *

Home at last, Dick had news that gave Maudie the peace she needed. 'Well, it's all over, old girl. We can relax now.'

'You mean he's been charged? What with? Wife beating? Threatening me?'

'Oh, much better than that. He'll go to trial for the murder of Verity Bourne.'

'But I thought you said it would be

hard to pin it on anyone, when there were no witnesses and no apparent motive.'

'The chap confessed, Maudie. It was almost as if he wanted it to be over, needed to get the whole sordid story off his chest. We got him a solicitor on Legal Aid, a nervous young fellow, still wet behind the ears, who warned him to sit still and say nothing, but he insisted on blurting it all out. It seems he first met Verity Bourne two years ago, when his ship docked at Liverpool.'

'Don't tell me he met her in a dockside pub! I wouldn't have thought that would have done her reputation much good, her being a school teacher.'

'No, he met her at the home of a shipmate, who is actually from Liverpool. This chap lives with his parents, as does his sister, who was a friend of Verity's. It was all quite respectable, other than the fact that Nate is a married man, of course. One thing led to another and they drifted into an affair.

'When he went back to sea he forgot about her; out of sight, out of mind, as they say, but when he next docked in

Liverpool she was waiting for him, and this time she put the pressure on. He found a letter waiting for him at the Seamen's Mission, in which she told him she was expecting his child and threatened to tell his wife unless he paid her 'a sum of money to be agreed on.' That, apparently, is when he went to her school, as Mrs Snead has suggested, intending to reason with her.'

'And we all know what form that reasoning would have taken!' Maudie said. 'What became of the child? Was she ever pregnant at all?'

'Lunney hasn't said. What is important, though, is that Verity followed this up by actually coming to Llandyfan, where she managed to wangle that job in the school. When he arrived home from his next voyage and learned from his son that his teacher was a Miss Bourne, he could hardly believe his ears.'

'And he was furious that she'd given his little boy the cane.'

'I doubt if that entered into it, Lunney being the brutal man that he is. But the fact that she'd actually dared to follow him here drove him crazy, as he put it.'

'I wouldn't have thought that he'd care if his wife learned about his affair with Verity,' Maudie said. 'He'd probably have told her she had to put up with it, and she'd have knuckled under, hoping he'd continue to provide for her and the boy.'

'I don't know about that, but he did admit that he was all set to sort out his problem, which took him up to knock on Mrs Peever's door. As you know she redirected him to Mrs Todd's, and when he got there both Verity and her landlady were at home. They couldn't hold a sensible conversation with the landlady's ears flapping, so Verity sent him away, saying he'd be in touch. She sent him a note by way of Eddie, asking him to meet her at the glebe, which she reckoned would be deserted at that time of day, with everyone being at school or at work.'

'And that's where it happened,' Maudie said, with a sigh. 'She walked right into it, didn't she.'

'I'm afraid she misjudged him badly. He says she flirted and led him on. Wanting him to leave his wife and return to Liverpool with her, until he suddenly 'saw red' as he put it. He says he noticed 'some sort of cloth scarf or tie' hanging from a gorse bush and on the spur of the moment he picked it up and wound it round her neck. 'She was so easy to kill,' he kept saying. 'She just gave a little whimper and then she was dead in my arms. I never meant to do it. She just drove me too far.' And that's the whole story, Maudie. He's been remanded in custody, and he'll come to trial in due course.'

For once Maudie could think of nothing to say. The man would hang, of course, and that terrible ending would cast a shadow over Edith Lunney and little Eddie for the rest of their lives.

31

Maudie was planning a very romantic evening. After the turmoil of recent weeks she felt that she and Dick deserved it. She had kept Charlie up all afternoon, playing with him so that now he was sound asleep in his cot, and with any luck he would stay that way until morning.

The rain was pelting down outside and there was a chill in the air, but Dick had a good fire going in the grate and the sitting room was cosy. Maudie had set the table with an embroidered cloth that had been a wedding present, and she had brought out the best china plates and two crystal wine glasses. Two fat candles stood in the middle of the table, and several more were lined up on the mantelpiece.

The aroma coming from the kitchen was enticing: lamb hotpot with dumplings, with a lemon meringue pie to follow. Rather homely food for a romantic tryst, she thought, but Dick would not have relished prawn cocktails or avocado pears and everyone knows that the way to a man's heart is through his stomach!

Maudie had shampooed her hair and brushed it until it shone. She had put on a pretty new dress, which was meant to be her 'for best' wear over the coming winter. A lightweight corduroy in light navy, with an overall pattern of little sprigs of flowers, pale blue and crimson. Gazing at herself in the bathroom mirror with approval, she carefully applied a coating of lipstick and wondered if another layer of mascara would be gilding the lily. A quick dab of perfume at her wrists and behind her ears, and she was ready for the fray.

She glanced at her wristwatch. She must go down in a minute and light the candles, and then it would be time to bring the casserole to the table and switch off the electric lights. She meant to find suitable music to play on the gramophone: *Smoke Gets in Your Eyes*, and perhaps Vera Lynn singing *The White Cliffs of Dover* for a bit of wartime nostalgia.

'You look good enough to eat,' Dick said when she came down the stairs, treading carefully in her high heels. 'Speaking of which, that hotpot smells marvellous. I'm hungry enough to eat a horse!'

'Coming right up!'

In the kitchen, with her good dress covered with an apron, Maudie lifted the casserole out of the oven and placed it carefully on a cork mat on the table. Should she have cooked greens to go with it, or were the carrots and onions she'd included in the succulent dish enough? *Oh, well; too late now! Go and light the candles, Maudie. Zero hour is here!*

She had a match in her hand when a thunderous knocking came at the door. Not again! 'Who on earth can that be? You're not expecting anyone, are you, Dick?'

'Of course not. This is our special night, old girl. Do you think I'd want to spoil that?' The pounding resumed. 'All right! Keep your hair on! I'm coming!'

A wild-eyed man stood on the door-step, his hair plastered down by the rain which was coming down harder than before.

'Are you the village constable?'

'Er no, not quite,' Dick began.

'But I stopped an old gaffer back there on the road and he said the constable lives here. My wife is about to have a baby and she needs help! I know coppers can deliver babies in an emergency and this is a bad one. The baby is coming and it's two months too soon. Are you sure you can't help?'

'I can do better than that,' Dick said. 'My wife is a midwife.'

Maudie appeared beside him, peering out into the rain. 'Have you called an ambulance?'

'I stopped at that phone box at the crossroads but the lines are down.'

'Never mind. You'd better bring her in and I'll take a look at her. Fetch the brolly, Dick and I'll go out and help her.'

The young woman was crammed into the cab of an ancient lorry, with only inches to spare between her swollen abdomen and the dashboard. The space behind the seat seemed to be full of ancient ironmongery: rusty tools, an enormous saw and a bucket of nails.

'I wouldn't care to deliver you in the middle of this lot,' Maudie said. 'Can you manage to climb down?'

'It's pouring out there,' the girl gasped.

'Never mind that. My husband will hold the umbrella over you. Now do come on. I'm getting a little damp myself.'

Once inside the house Maudie guided the girl to an armchair while Dick tried the telephone. 'Dead,' he said. 'The lines must be down all over the district because of the storm. Should I take the car and go to the ambulance station at Midvale, Maudie?'

'Before you do I'd better examine Mrs . . . I'm afraid I don't know your name.'

'Suzy Berton. Suzy with a zed. And that's my husband, Gary.'

'Well, Suzy with a zed, let me take a look at you, and then we can decide on our next move. Just stay there while I go and fetch my bag.'

Gary Berton still seemed agitated. 'What bag? What are you going to do?'

'I want an instrument called a pinard so I can listen to the baby's heartbeat, to make sure that all is well, and my sphygmomanometer to check your wife's blood pressure.'

'Of course all isn't well, you stupid woman! I told you, it's weeks too early. The baby can't live, I know that now, but I want my wife to be saved.'

Having undone the buttons of the woman's light raincoat, Maudie held her hand on the swollen abdomen. 'Calm down, Mr Berton. By my estimation this is a full-term baby, and right now it's eager to come into the world. You'll be a father before this night is out.'

'Full term? You don't know what you're talking about.'

Maudie smiled at her patient. 'What did your doctor tell you about your estimated date of delivery? Or it is a clinic nurse you've been seeing?'

'We haven't bothered with any of that,' Gary announced. 'Childbirth is a perfectly natural thing. Suzy can manage perfectly well without that sort of interference.'

Maudie did not reply, but her eyes

flashed momentarily and Dick decided to intervene. 'Do you live locally, Mr Berton? I don't believe we've met before.'

'We've only been here a couple of months. We're from Sheffield but we've rented a cottage up in the hills, a few miles from here, on a temporary basis, so I can get on with the novel I'm writing. I need the solitude, you see.'

'And you've chosen to participate in this perfectly natural event in the back of beyond, with no equipment and nobody to help?' Maudie spoke between gritted teeth. 'Maybe you want solitude but your wife needs proper care in a safe environment.'

'I told you, woman! She's not due for at least another two months. We'd have gone back to Sheffield in plenty of time for Suzy to give birth in some hospital there.'

'Well, you've left it a little late, Mr Berton. And I'll thank you not to call me woman!'

'What about the ambulance?' Dick asked. 'Shall I set off now?'

'I think not. By the time it gets here Mrs Berton will be well advanced in labour and she won't want to be jolted about. With all that rain the roads are likely to be full of potholes and the lane at the bridge could well be flooded by now. I say we should deliver the baby here and think about transportation to hospital later. And that being the case I shall need you here to fetch and carry for me, and to deal with Charlie if he wakes up.'

Outside, thunder began to roll. The light in the fixture overhead flickered and died. Dick stepped forward to light the candles on the mantel while Berton dithered helplessly in the background. 'What now, old girl?'

'You can go out to the scullery and fetch the hurricane lantern. Then go up to the attic and see if you can find that air mattress you had for camping, and while you're at it you can bring down Charlie's old Moses basket.'

Berton frowned. 'What do you want with some old air mattress, then? Don't you have a proper bed somewhere if my wife has to lie down?'

What did he mean by if? Maudie thought grimly. Did he think they were

285

going to bring the baby into the world with his wife sprawled in an armchair? She forced herself to speak politely.

'The power is off, Mr Berton, and I need to see what I'm doing! It's none too warm upstairs and once the baby gets here we mustn't let it get chilled.'

It might be an uncharitable thought, but Maudie wasn't about to let their bed be used for a messy home delivery. During the afternoon she had made it up afresh with her best linen sheets and spread a snowy white counterpane over the top, in anticipation of a happy ending to their romantic evening. Besides, the flickering fire would add to the light in the sitting room and their bedroom would be gloomy.

'The air mattress is in good condition, Mr Berton, and you can help by blowing it up.' *And that will put to good use some of that hot air you've been spouting*, she thought, grinning to herself. 'And why not take off that soaking overcoat? You're dripping all over the carpet. Dick will hang it in the scullery for you, and while you're at it, Dick you'd better put the dog out there as well.'

Rover was removed from the hearthrug and taken to the scullery by the scruff of his neck. As the door closed behind him he could be heard emitting soft moans of displeasure that his unfeeling owners ignored.

★　★　★

Maudie swung into action. First gathering a large enamel jug, a packet of soap flakes, a funnel and a rubber catheter, she escorted Suzy up to the bathroom. Having demanded to know why his wife was being taken upstairs, Berton delivered himself of the opinion that an enema was not only totally unnecessary but downright cruel, given his wife's condition. Maudie ignored him and told him to get on with blowing up the mattress. They left him huffing and puffing. She toyed with the idea of sending him off to Midvale, just to get him out of the way, but dismissed the thought. They didn't want an ambulance arriving just when they were in the thick of things, and besides, the vehicle might be needed elsewhere and they shouldn't keep it out of circulation.

'You'll have to excuse Gary,' Suzy said. 'He's all right, really. He just likes to be in control, you see, and me going into labour now has upset him.'

'That's quite all right, dear. I understand. Believe me, I've had plenty of experience dealing with distraught fathers-to-be. Now then, let's get this over with, shall we? Then we can make you comfortable downstairs and get on with the job.'

Hastily going through the trunk at the foot of their bed Maudie pulled out several tiny garments that had once belonged to Charlie: nightdresses that tied at the back, like a hospital gown in miniature. Seeing him now it was almost impossible to believe that he could ever have fitted into them. She added a tiny blanket and a knitted bonnet.

The airing cupboard on the landing yielded some elderly cotton sheets, shoved to the back in case they ever came in handy. Dick flatly refused to lie on sheets that had been turned 'sides to middle' but

Maudie had lived through two wars with shortages and rationing, and she had been unable to bring herself to throw them away. She completed the pile with two nappies; one of heavy terry cloth towelling, the smaller one of muslin.

'Anything else I can do?' Dick asked. 'Should I give Berton a hand with the mattress?'

'Let him carry on. Expectant fathers need their minds taking off what's happening. You can go and fetch that rubber sheet, though. It's in the cupboard in the scullery, and mind you don't let Rover out!'

Maudie went back upstairs to change out of her precious new frock. She took her uniform dress out of the wardrobe, and after a moment's thought put it back again. She expected to be lying on the sitting room carpet with her bottom in the air; an old pair of slacks might be preferable. She'd be wearing a gown over them anyway.

In due course Suzy lay on the makeshift bed with her husband hovering nearby. The Moses basket was stowed away under the table and the tiny garments were airing on the fire guard. Everything was going according to plan.

'Why don't you take Mr Berton into the kitchen, Dick? You may as well get your supper, and perhaps he could do with something as well.'

'What about you?'

'Just save me some of that casserole and I'll heat it up later.'

'Right-ho!'

* * *

An hour went by. Then two. Suzy's moans turned to screams. Berton rushed into the room, demanding to know what the matter was. Dick followed him in. 'Sorry, love! I couldn't stop him.'

'Why is she making such a fuss? Childbirth is a beautiful experience! Something must be going wrong and you don't know what you're doing!'

'Back into the kitchen, Mr Berton. You don't belong here.'

'Can't you see she's in pain, woman? Do something to help her! I knew we should have gone for that ambulance!'

Maudie was used to dealing with the shattered nerves of expectant fathers. 'Everything is quite all right, Mr Berton. Your wife is just entering the second stage of labour. It won't be much longer now.'

'What do you mean, second stage? She's not having twins, is she?'

'Labour consists of three parts, Mr Berton, but I can't stop to explain it to you now. If your wife had received proper antenatal care, as she should have done, these things would have been explained to you. As it is, I must ask you to go back to the kitchen and wait there until I call you.'

Time passed. 'I can see your baby's head, Suzy. Stop pushing. Pant, now, pant! Good girl. That's it, the head is born. Almost over now. I want you to give one enormous push. That's it. Keep going! Keep going!'

The baby slid into Maudie's waiting hands and immediately sent up a wail. 'There, now! No need to slap this one's bottom! You have a little girl, Suzy; a beautiful little daughter.'

Maudie applied clamps to the umbilical cord, cut it, wrapped the child in Charlie's baby blanket, and put the precious little bundle into her mother's waiting arms.

'She's perfect, Nurse. Absolutely perfect!'

'Babies always are,' Maudie said, smiling as she waited for the final stage of labour to be accomplished.

The door opened and the proud father appeared, swaying slightly. 'I'm afraid he's had that bottle of wine you bought to go with our special meal,' Dick whispered. 'I only offered him a little tot but he kept helping himself and there wasn't much I could do to stop him, short of bringing out the old handcuffs.'

The new father was sufficiently sober to be able to congratulate his wife and to peer at his daughter with apparent pleasure. His expression changed to horror when he noticed a basin that Maudie hadn't had time to cover up before he joined them.

'What on earth is that? Something is terribly wrong! Is Suzy bleeding to death?'

'It's only the placenta, Mr Berton; the

afterbirth. I've already checked it and everything seems to be in order, but they'll need to see it at the hospital, just to make sure.'

There was a crash, and a thud. Maudie turned round to see a dining chair upturned, and the patient's husband stretched out on the carpet.

'Did he hit his head on anything?' she asked Dick.

'No, but he went down like a ton of bricks. What should I do? I can't just leave him lying there.'

'Oh, throw a bucket of water over him!' Maudie said. She had had enough of Mr Gary Berton for one evening.

*　*　*

It was all over. Dick had driven Berton to the ambulance station at Midvale, and in due course Suzy and her baby were collected and taken to hospital after Maudie had graciously accepted the new mother's tearful thanks.

Rover was let out of the scullery, where Maudie wearily put a load of bloodstained sheets and towels to soak in the old galvanized tub. She was delighted to find that Dick had put a plate of hotpot to keep warm over a saucepan of simmering water and she tucked in heartily, blessing the fact that she had a gas cooker, for the electricity was not yet back on.

'I'll have my lemon meringue pie now,' she told Dick, who was warming the teapot to make a fresh brew. His face fell.

'Don't tell me you two scoffed the lot, Dick Bryant! I really fancied that!'

'But you love me anyway, don't you?' he pleaded.

'I suppose so, but mind you don't let it happen again!'

★　★　★

Their romantic evening had been snatched away from them, but perhaps after this they could go back to living a quiet life. Much had happened during the past few months. There had been the death of Verity Bourne, snatched away without living out her allotted span. To counteract it there had been the birth of baby girl Berton: a brand new life, full of promise. Birth and death, grief and joy; all part of our world as we know it. And Maudie Bryant, midwife, was at the centre of it all, and she was thankful for it.

'Shall we take our tea up to bed with us?' she asked.

Dick nodded. It had been a long, tiring day.

We do hope that you have enjoyed reading this large print book.

Did you know that all of our titles are available for purchase?

We publish a wide range of high quality large print books including:
Romances, Mysteries, Classics
General Fiction
Non Fiction and Westerns

Special interest titles available in large print are:
The Little Oxford Dictionary
Music Book, Song Book
Hymn Book, Service Book

Also available from us courtesy of Oxford University Press:
Young Readers' Dictionary
(large print edition)
Young Readers' Thesaurus
(large print edition)

For further information or a free brochure, please contact us at:
Ulverscroft Large Print Books Ltd.,
The Green, Bradgate Road, Anstey,
Leicester, LE7 7FU, England.
Tel: (00 44) 0116 236 4325
Fax: (00 44) 0116 234 0205

MISSION: TANK WAR

Michael Kurland

1960s: A small, oil-rich Arab nation is about to lose its status as a protectorate of Britain, and waiting in the wings to invade is a superior enemy force led by Soviet tanks. On a mission to stop them is debonair agent Peter Carthage and the men from War (Weapons Analysis and Research), Inc., a company with an ultra-scientific approach to warfare. How many men from War, Inc. does it take to stop an army of tanks? Six — plus one beautiful, plucky young British woman determined to rescue a kidnapped brother.

GIVE THE GIRL A GUN

Richard Deming

Manville Moon is a private investigator. On a night out with his girlfriend Fausta Moreni, the lovely owner of the El Patio Café, a group of customers invites them both to a private party at an inventor's home, to celebrate the launch of a business venture based on his new device. But soon after their arrival, the inventor is shot dead by an unseen assailant. Police suspicion quickly falls on the boyfriend of one of the guests, and Moon is hired to prove his innocence — plunging him and Fausta into deadly danger . . .